"What about you?"

Her eyes widened. "What about me?"

"Why don't you pretend to be my girlfriend while you're in Dunn? You're the perfect choice. We like spending time together, and it would make sense that we met. Our siblings are living together. Plus—"

She shot her arm out toward Isaac to shake his hand. He accepted, amused and damn pleased when she gave his palm a hardy pump. "Sign me up, Isaac Dunn. I'll be your girlfriend."

"All right then." His girlfriend problems were officially over. And, if he had his way, he wouldn't mind adding some real affection to the list. It'd been a while since he'd had a woman in his arms—and a woman like Meghan, well, he'd never seen her like.

She was right. This was going to be *fun*.

* * *

Million-Dollar Consequences by Jessica Lemmon is part of The Dunn Brothers series.

Dear Reader,

In Dunn, Virginia, anything is possible.

Meghan Squire's ultimate fantasy has come true. Not only does she finally meet the celebrity she had a crush on during her childhood, but he has also agreed to be interviewed for her podcast. Oh, and he's asking her to pretend to be his fiancée for a few months' time... *Whaaat?*

Identical twin and former child star Isaac Dunn has returned after spending years out of the spotlight. The show that put him on the map has been rebooted for a reunion series, marking the start of his epic comeback. Recruiting smart, sassy Meghan to pose as his fiancée is his best idea yet. Finally, he has his life under control. Until he doesn't...

Their fake relationship includes some very real heat! Can they make this "temporary" coupling into something more?

I invite you to sit back and enjoy the show, both the scripted one being filmed in town, and the sparks flying between Meghan and Isaac as they try to figure out how this whole "love" thing works.

Read for fun!

xo,

Jessica Lemmon

PS: For book updates and behind-the-scenes fun, visit www.jessicalemmon.com.

JESSICA LEMMON

MILLION-DOLLAR CONSEQUENCES

HARLEQUIN®
DESIRE™

Recycling programs
for this product may
not exist in your area.

ISBN-13: 978-1-335-73568-3

Million-Dollar Consequences

Copyright © 2022 by Jessica Lemmon

For questions and comments about the quality of this book,
please contact us at CustomerService@Harlequin.com.

Harlequin Enterprises ULC
22 Adelaide St. West, 41st Floor
Toronto, Ontario M5H 4E3, Canada
www.Harlequin.com

Printed in U.S.A.

A former job-hopper, **Jessica Lemmon** resides in Ohio with her husband and rescue dog. She holds a degree in graphic design, which is currently gathering dust in an impressive frame. When she's not writing supersexy heroes, she can be found cooking, drawing, drinking coffee (okay, wine) and eating potato chips. She firmly believes God gifts us with talents for a purpose, and with His help, you can create the life you want.

Jessica is a social media junkie who loves to hear from readers. You can learn more at jessicalemmon.com.

Books by Jessica Lemmon

Harlequin Desire

Dynasties: Beaumont Bay

Second Chance Love Song
Good Twin Gone Country

The Dunn Brothers

Million-Dollar Mix-Up
Million-Dollar Consequences

Visit her Author Profile page at Harlequin.com, or jessicalemmon.com, for more titles.

You can also find Jessica Lemmon on Facebook, along with other Harlequin Desire authors, at Facebook.com/harlequindesireauthors!

One

Dunn, Virginia.

Isaac Dunn's twin brother had gone and had a town named after him.

Not on purpose. Max, in his effort to escape the Hollywood spotlight, had attempted to hide out by purchasing this mountain town. But as per his usual, surly Max was beloved by everyone. Isaac, given his relation to Max, had been accepted by The *Dunnians* on sight.

The rift that had occurred between them after their successful TV show ended had healed. But the scar was still a visible one. Isaac and Max had always been a unit—in the womb and well into their twenties, before Max left Hollywood. Once Max stated he'd wanted nothing to do with the show, Isaac had taken it personally. It'd felt like Max had wanted nothing to do with Isaac, either.

Over the years, they'd patched things up for the most part. Isaac had shot commercials and had filmed a few television pilots that hadn't led anywhere. Now, though…

Now was different.

Not only had Isaac been given a second chance at fame, but he was starring in the reboot of the very show that had skyrocketed him into the public spotlight.

He was in the process of a second big break. Temporarily living in the same town as his once estranged brother, Isaac was healing those past hurts, one filming day at a time. The town loved him, his brother and he were growing closer by the day, and the cast and crew had been nothing but supportive.

Everything was finally falling into place, piece by piece. This whole do-over thing wasn't something he would half-ass.

He stepped around the extras on set and waved to Ashley Lee, director of the *Brooks Knows Best* reboot. She hadn't been around when both Isaac and Max had acted in the show decades ago, taking turns playing the same young character. Now Danny Brooks was all grown up and being played by just one of them—Isaac.

"Nice work today," she told him.

At five-ten, Ashley wasn't dainty by any stretch of the imagination. She was wildly confident, despite *Brooks Knows Best* being her directorial debut. Even Isaac had suffered a bout of nerves before reprising his role as Danny Brooks, and had absconded to his private island to prepare alone.

"Thanks, Ash."

She took a look around before she lowered her voice. "Cecil is asking about your girlfriend. He maintains that the public needs to see her, and soon. He's worried about bad publicity."

"I thought all publicity was good publicity," Isaac replied.

The girlfriend announcement, meant to distract from another PR issue, had caused a ruckus. That white lie had been chasing him for months.

He couldn't tell anyone the truth, save his agent and his brother, who already knew: there *was* no girlfriend. He'd made her up to save himself from a whole lot of explaining earlier this year.

"You know my father-in-law." Ashley shrugged. "Only good publicity is good publicity. He is trying to keep the show in a positive light so we can soar to number one the week it releases on the streaming service. Every detail counts."

Isaac did, indeed, know her father-in-law. The producer was white-haired, hot-tempered, and rarely smiled. Cecil Fowler had been intimidating when Isaac was a child actor. Not as much now, but it was in Isaac's best interest to keep Cecil smiling.

All he had to do was find a woman who could play the role of a lifetime: his girlfriend. Confessing he'd made her up would send Cecil off the deep end and topple the pile of carefully stacked blocks before Isaac climbed it to the top. Isaac was going to reclaim what he'd lost. Success or bust, no exceptions.

"She might be able to stop by during filming," he told Ash with a smile. "I'll check with her."

"I want to meet her. Not for publicity reasons but to see if you managed to find a nice girl."

"You bet." He'd like to meet her, too. "See you tomorrow."

So far, scrounging up a girlfriend—even a fake one—had been an impossible task. It'd started when he and his agent had pulled a fast one on the public, and pretended to be dating. The truth came out, which would have cast a shadow over the reprisal of *Brooks Knows Best* if Isaac hadn't thought fast. He'd concocted a story about Kendall covering for the woman he was *actually* in love with. The attention had then shifted from the lie about dating Kendall—who had only pretended to date Isaac because the public had seen her with Max—and on to the woman Isaac had yet to introduce to the public.

It'd been too much negative attention for Cecil. The aging producer knew what Isaac knew—that the public could be fickle. At the height of cancel culture, the show could tank before they were done filming, if they weren't careful.

Since Isaac's top goal was to ride his comeback wave to a larger role on a blockbuster film, he was determined to find a solution both he and Cecil could live with.

Isaac would find a girlfriend. *Somewhere.*

With filming wrapped for the day, he stepped out

of the coffee shop into the sunshine. Virginia couldn't touch California for quantity of sunshiny days, but Isaac liked it here.

Max had accidentally reinvigorated the mountain town when all he'd been trying to do was escape LA. With Max living on the opposite side of the country, Isaac had felt as if he'd been missing a limb. It was good to be near his brother again.

Isaac had once been half of a whole, working in a career that had gone up, up, up. He'd made the mistake of believing success would last forever. His role in *Brooks Knows Best*, which was filming here in Dunn, was his best shot at reclaiming that success, and healing his relationship with Max.

"Are you…are you Isaac Dunn?" a hesitant, but excited voice asked.

He turned to find a young girl, maybe fifteen or sixteen, hands clutched under her chin, eyes wide. She was too young to have watched the show when it originally aired, but the publicity around the reboot had drawn in both old and fresh crowds. Her mom, he assumed, stood behind her. Closer to Isaac's age and watching him with the same starstruck admiration, if a bit more reserved than her daughter's.

"I am." He turned on a grin and took the notebook the young girl offered. He wasn't approached on the street on a regular basis back in LA, but here, where the show was being filmed, that hadn't been the case. Fans had flocked to the luxe mountain town of Dunn in the hopes for a peek at the formerly famous cast.

"I have a pen," the girl's mother said, her smile shaking at the edges. Isaac chatted long enough to learn their names and sign an autograph, and then posed for a photo.

All in a day's work.

He angled toward his rented apartment, his home away from home as of two weeks ago, perched above a deli and furnished to the nines. He didn't make it off the curb before his phone rang.

"Kendall," he answered his agent's call. His agent, his brother's girlfriend, probably his future sister-in-law—he wasn't sure what to call her now. Surely a proposal was forthcoming. Thing was, he didn't know if Kendall or Max would be the one to pop the question.

"Hi!" she chirped. "Are you done filming?"

"Yep, just wrapped."

"I know we said seven, but we're at Rocky's early. Is it too soon for you to come out?"

"Not at all. I can be there in five minutes."

"Great! We're all here, in the corner by the patio."

Isaac said goodbye and pocketed his phone, tracking up the sidewalk in the direction of the sports bar rather than toward his apartment. Rocky's was outfitted with plenty of noisy televisions and *bing*-ing arcade games. The cast and crew had frequented the bar after filming for the day, so he'd been there more than a few times. Today, though, he was going to meet Kendall's baby sister.

Evidently, his agent's sister was a huge fan of the show, and hoping that an interview with Isaac would build up her podcast following. Like he'd been gracious to the young girl asking for an autograph, he didn't mind showing up to help a struggling podcaster, either. Kendall had worked hard to boost Isaac's career—including that brief stint posing as his girlfriend—so he figured he owed her.

The short walk was scenic, the backdrop of tall pines and mountaintops a view straight out of a Bob Ross painting. Inside, he scanned the restaurant for his bearded brother, his agent and her younger sister. He skipped over a trio in the back corner, only to snap his head around for a second take. That was Max, all right, and Kendall. The woman tossing her head back and laughing, red lipstick highlighting her sensual mouth, was *not* the college-age student he'd assumed she would be.

Kendall's reference to her "baby" sister had him picturing a young girl like the one he'd just encountered. This blonde, wearing a floral dress that hugged her very womanly curves, was closer to his age than he'd previously assumed.

"Isaac!" Kendall waved him over. When he arrived, she gestured to the beautiful creature on the opposite side of the table. "This is my sister, Meghan."

Meghan's hazel eyes twinkled as she flipped the length of her blond hair over one shoulder. Her cheeks stained a soft pink, her smile tenuous and completely captivating.

"The podcaster," Isaac finally managed. He hadn't expected a woman half as stunning as Meghan. He hadn't expected the blast of sexual awareness, either, but it saturated the air around him. So thick he swore he could taste the honey-sweet richness on his tongue.

"Oh my God, it's really you." Her mouth split into an adorably crooked grin, showing off straight white teeth. Dark lashes batted as she stared up at him as if in awe. "I thought meeting Max was cool, but…wow. Isaac Dunn."

He had to laugh. He'd been flattered plenty in his career, but never had he remembered the answering drop in his gut when it'd happened.

"Thanks a lot," Max grumbled.

"You know what I mean." Meghan waved off Max's complaint as if she was already used to his surliness.

Isaac sat in the empty chair next to Meghan, aware of how good she smelled, and the heat radiating from her knee to his, mere inches apart under the table. He was also aware he was staring at her but couldn't seem to keep from it.

"We're not going to be able to stay," Kendall interrupted.

"No?" Isaac's shoulders dropped. He would have liked to talk to Meghan a while longer. "What's up?"

"Video conference call. What else?" His agent rolled her eyes. Isaac knew she wasn't the least bit inconvenienced by working remote. Kendall loved her job as a talent agent. She might've left LA, but she hadn't slowed down a bit. Once Max had asked her to move in with him, she'd left California as soon as possible.

Ah, love.

After the truth had come out about Max and Kendall being an *actual* couple, Isaac had blurted out the girlfriend "confession." He'd had to tell the talk show host something after Max had burst onto the stage and claimed Kendall for himself. For a guy who shunned the spotlight, his brother had bathed in it for the woman he loved.

Isaac was happy for them. He'd have to be dead not to feel a tingle of warmth from their story.

"Do you mind taking a car back to the cabin?" Kendall asked Meghan.

"Not at all." She smiled at Isaac. "If you don't mind hanging out with a rabid superfan for a while?"

Hell, no, he didn't mind. He spread his hands and grinned. "Rabid superfans are my specialty."

Two

Lord, but the man is attractive.

Which Meghan should have expected, since he looked, well, *identical* to his *identical* twin, Max. When she'd arrived in Dunn to stay with her sister and the famous Max Dunn, Meghan thought she'd been prepared to meet his twin. She'd been begging her sister, aka Isaac's agent, to introduce them for forever, and now it was finally happening! Meghan was a bundle of excited energy masquerading as easygoing.

Identical twin or no, Isaac wasn't a carbon copy of his brother in every way. His smile was full and generous, where Max's smile—if he *deigned* to smile—was hidden beneath a thick, well-groomed beard. Isaac wasn't clean-shaven but his facial hair was bad-boy scruff rather than mountain-man beard.

"Does the show require you to have a beard, or was that your choice?"

"Are these the sort of hard-hitting questions I can expect from your podcast?" His grin persisted, and she thought she might swoon right off her chair. Not only because the most beautiful man in the world seemed as captivated by her as she was by him, but also because of those eyes. Similar to Max's, Isaac's irises were a stunning shade of blue, but if Max's eyes held the same gilded golden edge around the pupil, Meghan had missed it.

"I'm just getting warmed up." Her podcast, *Superfan TV*, had seen a bit of success, but she hoped to gain more after she interviewed the hot twin brothers whose childhood show was making a comeback.

"All right, then. It's a requirement. They wanted to drive home the idea that Danny Brooks is grown up."

She'd say. Her eyes traversed over rounded shoulders and the T-shirt hugging the telltale bulges of impressive biceps. He wasn't the kid a few years older than her with the teenage swagger. Isaac Dunn was one hundred percent man.

"Not that he can grow a full beard," Max interjected, reminding her that he was still here. Meghan should probably save her swooning for later. Like, say, after her sister and Max left. "He busted his chin falling off a stage when he was seven. You can see the scar if you look closely."

Isaac gave a smirking Max a withering glare, but it didn't reach his eyes. Isaac seemed the more amenable of the two of them. Sort of like her and Kendall.

Though her five-years-older sister wasn't intense, Kendall had been sad and serious for a number of years. Far too many of them. It was so good to see her happy again.

Contrarily, Meghan believed that joy was her compass. She prided herself in maintaining her childlike wonder, in staying curious and letting life surprise her. Sure, that sort of whimsical way of living had been hard on her bank account at times, and *yes*, she might own a time-share she shouldn't have purchased and couldn't get out of owning, but at least she was having fun. If you weren't having fun, what was the point of doing anything?

"Tomorrow is the big day! Brothers reunite on set," Kendall said to Isaac and Max collectively. "Are you excited?"

The unthinkable had happened when Max had agreed to a small part on the show. Kendall had told Meghan that Max was dead set against appearing in front of a camera again. Over the last few months, thanks to Kendall's talent agent voodoo, Max had been convinced to join the cast.

When there was a lull between the brothers, Kendall answered for them. "Well, I'm excited. Your fans are going to go nuts."

Isaac turned to Meghan and once again she was basking in his complete attention. After watching him on television for years, and developing a debilitating crush on his character, it was thrilling to be this close to him. Too bad he had a girlfriend.

Her heart sunk at the reminder. Great looking, smiley

and charming, it wasn't surprising to hear that Isaac wasn't single. He'd yet to be photographed with the mystery woman. Not that Meghan had thought she'd a shot at dating him herself, but the fantasy bubble had popped when she'd heard he was taken.

Sigh.

"Sorry to run off." Kendall shouldered her purse and stood from the table. "Tomorrow we can record the podcast at Max's place."

"*Our* place, California." Max wrapped an arm around Kendall's waist. Between the gooey look he gave her and that adorable nickname, Meghan had no doubt how much he loved her sister.

"Our place." Kendall, peering up at her beloved through her lashes, weaved her fingers with his. With one last wave, they made their way out of the restaurant.

Meghan turned back to the younger-by-seventy-two-seconds Dunn. Even with a background of noisy sports on television and the flashing lights of the pinball machine in the corner, Isaac commanded attention. With his longer hair, scanter beard and easygoing attitude, he was every bit the rom-com star.

A waiter stopped by to take their drink orders. She ordered the same beer as Isaac, earning her a raised eyebrow. "Beer girl?"

"I am not picky when it comes to drinks. I blame college."

"What'd you major in?"

"Fashion. Not that I finished my degree."

"You're very well-dressed. The classes you did take paid off."

She ran a hand down her floral dress. She was tempted to feel flattered but then reminded herself that his charm was likely practiced.

"Where are you visiting from?"

"North Carolina."

"Apartment? House? Husband? Kids?" He rattled off the questions, and for a beat she wondered if he was trying to suss out her single status. But then, why would he? He was hiding a girlfriend somewhere. One who must be the most understanding woman on the planet to let him pretend to date Kendall for a stint.

"I rent a farmhouse. It's big for just me, but I like the space. Beautiful sunrises in the morning. Not that I am awake to see them. No kids. No husband. Just a barn cat that wanders around the property, but he isn't mine."

She stated the facts evenly rather than allow the emotions lurking behind them to enter her voice. She hadn't always lived in a rented farmhouse with beautiful sunrises. Once, she'd shared an apartment with her boyfriend, Lane. He'd highlighted her faults, frequently. He saw her as flighty at best, irresponsible at worst. His needling—about her lack of focus and her inability to put him first—had taken a chunk out of her confidence.

"…that was the only time I'd been," Isaac was saying.

She felt her cheeks grow warm. She'd spaced out while he was talking. *Way to make a great first impression!*

"I'm so sorry. I was thinking about something, and I missed what you said. I do that sometimes. It's embarrassing and irritating. I don't have a diagnostic excuse. I'm pretty sure I'm just—"

"Fine." He placed his hand over hers gently. It was the briefest touch but soothed her to the soles of her feet. "You're totally fine." He was still smiling and didn't appear irritated or frustrated the way Lane had been with her at times. "I was saying I've been to Raleigh to visit a friend, but that was the only time I'd been to your fine state."

"Oh. Well, it's lovely. Virginia is nice, too. I can't believe Kendall left California for the East Coast, but I'm so glad she did. I missed her." Their beers were delivered, and they clinked the drafts together before each taking a sip. Even though the alcohol had yet to hit her bloodstream, she instantly relaxed. "How long are you staying in Virginia?"

"Until the shoot's over. I love California. You've been there, I assume. To visit Kendall?"

"A few times." Plane tickets were costly, so she hadn't gone as much as she would have liked. "I don't mind a city atmosphere, but LA is overwhelming. I prefer it here."

"Yeah." He turned his head to look out the window where people strolled by on the sidewalk next to a not-so-busy street. "It's very…Max."

Was it her, or did a hint of strain creep into his voice when he said his brother's name? She knew what had happened between them only as far as the internet had reported. It would be rude to bring up gossip, though.

"Are you and Max close?" Oops. So much for that

plan. She opened her mouth to apologize but Isaac answered her question before she could.

"We're getting there." He squinted one eye and in a teasing tone accused, "Is this why you want to interview us? To dig up the rift we had years ago?"

"No! Oh, gosh, no. I wouldn't do that."

"Teasing." He touched her lightly on the hand again. His blue gaze held hers, the air thickening between them. Just as she was reminding herself that he was taken, he asked, "Do you want to stay for dinner?"

Isaac watched Meghan's reaction carefully, unsure if he'd overstepped. "Professionally, of course."

He'd do well to remember the world believed he had a girlfriend. The last thing he needed were rumors bouncing around that he was cheating on his imaginary girlfriend.

"I'd love to." Meghan's crooked smile returned. She was far bubblier than Kendall, which he preferred. Meghan liked to laugh and talk. She was adorably starstruck, which he knew how to handle. He was enormously attracted to her, which he *normally* knew how to handle.

He supposed she could be playing up her personality to make him feel comfortable enough so that she could draw out his secrets, but he doubted it. Kendall was his agent. She would never set him up for a fall, especially with her own sister.

"Dinner with *the* Isaac Dunn," Meghan murmured, before her mouth fell open in what looked like shock. "I'm sorry. That was— I didn't mean—"

"I've never been a *the* before. I like it, but why don't you call me Isaac from now on." He picked up a menu. "What do you want to eat?"

"In a place like this? Fattening, fried appetizers is the only way to go."

"Beer and fried food. You live on the edge, Meghan Squire."

Her teeth speared a plump red bottom lip and parts of him that had no business stirring stirred. Not only did he have to keep up the pretense of a girlfriend, but this was Kendall's sister. He couldn't make a move if he wanted to. What a shame.

When the waiter came around, he ordered an assortment of apps for them. Meghan tacked on a salad to "even the score." He did the same. While they forked through their greens, he quizzed her some more. "When did you start your podcast?"

"About three years ago. I used to record a show a month, but now it's once a week."

"That's a lot. And every episode is about television shows?"

"Yeah. I'm kind of a junkie. I have recorded at least a dozen episodes about *Brooks Knows Best.*"

"Wow. Big fan, then." He stabbed another bite.

"The biggest." She popped a cherry tomato into her mouth. "I bet you hear that all the time."

"I do. More often *not* in reference to the show." He winked and let the comment hang. Her top teeth pulled her bottom lip again. *Interesting.* "Are Max and I your first celebrity interviews?"

"No. But you are the most famous. A lot of actors

who are former sitcom stars don't stay in the spotlight long after. It's a tough business. I'm sure you know that."

Boy, did he. Once Max literally went in a different direction, Isaac had been on his own auditioning for commercials, pilots and the ultimate: *film*. He'd had moderate success, but nothing like being asked to come back to *Brooks Knows Best*.

If ever he'd been primed to make a comeback, now was his chance. Already the buzz surrounding the show's popularity had ushered in more offers for him. Kendall had been turning down less lucrative parts on his behalf, thanks to his current schedule.

"When we record the podcast, I'll ask questions about the show and the reunion with your fellow actors. About Ashley Lee's directorial debut." Meghan leaned forward and lowered her voice. "I love her. Tell me she's as amazing as she seemed when she starred in *Lamb's Wool*."

Isaac smiled at the reference to Ashley's starring role. A former actress, she'd been nominated for awards and had landed on every talk show in the country. She'd walked away from what could have been a lucrative acting career to direct a reboot of a TV show. Isaac couldn't personally understand, but he admired the hell out of her for going after what she wanted.

He leaned close and gave Meghan the answer she was hoping for, which also happened to be the truth. "She's better."

Meghan's eyes twinkled. In that moment, he had the irrational urge to press his lips to hers. He'd never experienced such an immediate attraction to anyone.

"So, the interview," she continued, interrupting the sizzling tension between them. "Is there anything you need me to know beforehand?"

He sat back in his chair as several plates of fried mozzarella sticks, jalapeño bites and onion straws were delivered and divided. He reminded himself that the show—and the show's reputation—was the most important thing in his life. Meghan was giving him a chance to talk about it, and he wasn't going to miss the opportunity to have her paint him in the best light possible.

"The only thing you need to know," he said as he dragged a mozzarella stick through a ramekin of marinara, "is that Danny Brooks is back and better than ever."

Three

"You've done this a million times. It's no big deal. You've got this." Meghan blew out a breath and checked her microphones for the thirtieth time. She'd set up her laptop, three microphones—Max and Kendall were going to have to share one, but she didn't think they'd mind—and coasters where everyone could set their water glasses. She'd learned a long time ago that the mics picked up on the *clunk* sound of glasses hitting the table if she didn't pad the blow.

"Impressive, little sister." Kendall entered the kitchen by way of the patio. She'd scrubbed the grill to ready it for steaks, and a portobello mushroom for Meghan, since she wasn't a meat-eater. Kendall set the brush and spatula in the sink and washed her hands while she spoke. "Are you nervous?"

"A little." No sense in lying.

"Don't let Isaac intimidate you."

"He doesn't intimidate me."

Kendall gave her a look communicating that she knew Meghan was lying, or at least exaggerating.

"*Fine.* But he only intimidates me because I've watched him on television so much, I feel like a younger version of me when I see him. I don't know the grown-up version of him."

"The grown-up version of both of you are success-ful and kind and funny. You will do great. You said dinner went well last night, right?"

"He is really nice." What a lame descriptor. He'd set her at ease more than once when he'd noticed her nerves getting the best of her. But tonight was differ-ent. He was on her turf. Sort of. This was Max's house, but once she hit the record button, Meghan would be in charge.

"I never would have guessed you'd like doing this." Kendall touched one of the microphones. "You're like a DJ."

"I'm more like a radio version of Oprah. It's my job to learn more about the entertainment my viewers and I consumed while we were growing up. There is a reason it resonated with us, and I'm on a mission to uncover why."

"And here I thought *Superfan TV* was a fun side gig while you worked for Monroe Advertising."

Where she'd met her ex-boyfriend Lane. Meghan had been impressed by his air of success and power. Only after she'd moved in with him did she learn how set in his ways he was. He had been closing in on forty years old to her naive twenty-five at the time. He'd made her feel more like a problem that needed solving than a girlfriend he loved.

When things had ultimately imploded, she'd returned to her old friend, *Brooks Knows Best*. When their brother died, Meghan had lost herself in the show while Kendall had shut down in her bedroom. *Brooks* had been there for Meghan during her darkest times, so it wasn't any wonder why she held Isaac in such high regard.

After the breakup with Lane, she'd begun the podcast on a whim. She'd landed a small amount of advertising money. Her audience had grown and then slumped, only to grow and slump again. It hadn't been an easy road, but she'd made it work. And it'd allowed her to leave Monroe Advertising. With a few odd jobs and the podcast, Meghan had found a way to support herself without a full-time job or Lane.

"It was a side gig at first," Meghan said. "But then I learned that nothing made me happier than talking about the Brooks family. Whenever I was down, they lifted me up. They were always there for me."

"And I wasn't." Kendall's eyebrows bent in regret.

"I don't think that." She placed her hand on her sister's arm. "Quinton's death was hard on everyone. You dealt with losing him as best as you could."

Happiness used to fog her childhood home until their brother died. After, it'd been like the warm fires of joy had been smothered with a damp tarp. Since Meghan hadn't wanted to suffocate in the smoke, she had crawled out and found her own version of happiness. Their parents had been focused on Kendall at the time, as well they should have been. Meghan hadn't resented her sister for needing her parents more back then.

Although, she sometimes wondered if they had paid her more attention when she was younger, if she'd be as responsible as Kendall. Meghan wasn't purposefully careless or forgetful, but she'd had her fair share of fuckups over the last nine years. Growing up had been like a game of Chutes and Ladders. Each time she climbed, she slid down only to have to climb again. Rinse and repeat.

"In a way, Danny Brooks saved me." Meghan shrugged.

"Which Danny Brooks?" Kendall teased.

"I have always been able to tell Max and Isaac apart. Even on the show where they were supposed to be the same person."

"Max was the broodier of the two," Kendall concluded.

And Isaac was the hotter one.

Meghan kept that thought to herself. Good thing, too, because a second later the front door opened and in walked Max and Isaac, in the middle of whatever conversation they'd been having in the car.

"Ashley is right," Max was saying.

"She usually is. That's what makes her a great director." Isaac shut the door behind him as Max went to Kendall to kiss her hello. Isaac didn't sweep in and kiss Meghan—more's the pity—but he did grin and walk directly to her. If he didn't have a girlfriend, she might let herself believe that'd meant something. But then, he was an amazing actor. He could turn on the charm when he wanted.

"Give me five?" Max asked Meghan.

She was so stunned when he waited for her to respond, it took her a second to answer. "Five minutes? Sure. Yes."

He dipped his chin before heading upstairs. Kendall excused herself to help him change and ran after him.

Isaac took the chair next to Meghan, his eyes on the staircase. "Think they're doing it? In five minutes?"

"God knows they haven't stopped since I arrived. You should hear the excuses. *I have to brush my teeth. Want to brush your teeth, Max? I can't find my sneakers. Kendall, can you help me find my sneakers?*'" Meghan grinned when Isaac laughed. He had a great laugh. Low and inviting. "I reminded her this morning that I'm not twelve years old, and I know exactly what they're doing."

"Let me guess. It had nothing to do with teeth-brushing or sneaker-finding." He grinned.

"I highly doubt it."

Ten minutes later, Max jogged downstairs behind a rosy-cheeked Kendall. Meghan prepped her guests, reassuring them that if they said something they didn't mean, it could be edited out. She then gave them a rough idea of the types of questions she'd be asking, though she didn't go into great detail. She liked authentic moments on her show. Too much preparation endangered the spontaneity.

The moment she hit Record on her laptop, she slipped into professional mode. Using the notes on her screen, she quizzed Kendall and Max and Isaac alike, focusing on the show and the cast's reunion. She asked her sister if she found it awkward representing both brothers, one of those brothers being her boyfriend. Kendall had laughed and stated that she was more than happy to have both Dunn brothers under her charge.

While she was about to burst from curiosity, Meghan didn't ask Isaac to divulge the whereabouts of his girlfriend. She mentioned his free time and asked how he spent it, leaving a wide enough gap for him to mention his mystery woman if he wanted to. When he didn't, she opted to take the high road.

Once she had a good amount of content, and she was confident she could whittle down the interview to an hour-long show, she pressed the stop button and took her headphones off. "That's it, you guys. Great job."

"Good. I need a beer." Max stood. "Anyone else?"

"Wine," Kendall said. "I'll get it."

"Beer is fine," Isaac and Meghan answered in unison. They met each other's gazes for an extended beat.

Isaac shook his head. "I like you more and more every second I'm around you."

Meghan couldn't help it, she floated on that compliment to the patio after she and Isaac had their beer bottles in hand. Settling onto wicker chairs facing an autumn mountain view, they sipped their drinks. Isaac let out a sigh.

"Long day?" she prompted.

"Yes, but a fun one. It's not every day I can work with my brother."

What a great answer. She could return the compliment he gave her a few minutes ago. The more she was around him, the more she liked him. "And now one of my favorite actors is preparing my dinner. Incredible."

She turned her head to watch her sister and Max through the slatted blinds in the kitchen window. They were side by side at the countertop, sprinkling seasoning on meat and mushrooms alike. Kendall smiled and Max leaned down to kiss her, and then, holding their seasoned-covered fingers out to their sides, they made out for a moment.

"You're right," Isaac said. "They don't stop. Have you thought about renting your own place in town to avoid them?"

"God, yes." She wasn't about to tell him why she hadn't, which was that Million-Dollar Mountain and the town of Dunn only offered incredibly expensive rooms for rent. "Can I ask you something I didn't ask on the podcast?"

"Uh-oh. Here I was convinced you weren't the bloodthirsty type." He craned one eyebrow as he raked a longer bit of hair from his forehead. He was too attractive for words.

"I won't tell anyone. I just want to know for my own fangirl heart."

"When you talk like that you weaken my resolve, Squire."

It was the first time he'd addressed her by her last name. Paired with his teasing tone and a knee-weakening half smile, she nearly forgot the question she wanted to ask.

"I'm an open book." Belying his words, he folded his arms over his chest and straightened his back. Rather than point out he looked more like a *closed* book, she asked the question that had been on her mind for months.

"It's about the woman who stole your heart while you were vacationing on your private island. You'd mentioned you wouldn't reveal her identity until she's ready, but can you tell me anything about her?"

Four

You mean like the fact that she doesn't exist?

He'd been impressed during the podcast interview both by Meghan's professionalism and the way she gave him ample room to answer her questions. She hadn't overprepared, either, letting them go off on miniature tangents if the topic warranted. She also hadn't pried.

This off-the-record question, however, had gone for his jugular.

"I want to know for me," she insisted. "This might be awkward to admit, but I feel like I've known you my whole life. I have followed you on the show, beyond the show and now for the reunion of the show. I know I'm not the only fan who wants Isaac Dunn to have a happily-ever-after. People are rooting for you."

While she talked, an idea took root. It was so perfect; he couldn't believe it hadn't occurred to him before. He needed a pretend girlfriend to introduce to the fans and paparazzi in town, and to his grouchy producer and curious director. He'd been stalling until he found a candidate to stand in as that woman. Right about now, he thought he could be looking right at her.

Why not Meghan? The press didn't know her—even with her moderate podcast success. Plus, given that she recorded podcasts for a living, who's to say she hadn't been recording her show from his private island? In theory, anyway.

Plus, she was his agent's sister, which was looking less like a reason not to pursue her and more like the perfect reason to do it. Him being introduced to Meghan wasn't far-fetched, and Kendall fake-dating him to cover for her own sister made complete sense. And, he continued mentally building his case, Meghan was in Dunn at the same time as him. She could pop by the studio and meet Cecil and Ashley, who would no doubt fall in love with her the way they'd believed Isaac had.

Meghan Squire was bright and fun and sweet. She was the perfect fake girlfriend. If she agreed to step in, his search would be over. Better yet, there would be nothing to distract him from what mattered: his second big career break. He was ready to have complete control over his life again. It'd been a long time coming.

"Anyway, I'll stop rambling. I've made my plea. Tell me or don't tell me." She squinted one eye, looking as cute as ever. "But if you do tell me, I swear I won't tell a soul."

"I have a proposition for you, Squire."

Honey-brown eyebrows met over innocent hazel eyes. "I beg your pardon?"

He lowered his voice to make the offer, though his brother and Kendall would find out about it soon enough. "The truth is, there is no mystery woman. I didn't fall in love with anyone on my island. I was there, alone, prepping for my role. When I came home, I found out that the world thought Kendall and I were an item. What else was I supposed to do?"

"You…you lied about having a girlfriend?"

"I *distracted* Wendi Watts on her gossip-rag talk show by saying I had a girlfriend. You saw Max storm onto her show to claim your sister. I had to think fast and divert attention somehow."

"Oh." Meghan's face fell. Disappointment washed over her features. He could expect a similar reaction if he admitted the truth to the very large *Brooks Knows Best* fan base. He couldn't admit he'd lied to them twice. His reputation, the show's reputation and his very future depended on him finding a woman to fake it with him. Someone who understood his motivation and who believed the best of him. Someone like Meghan Squire.

"What about you?"

Her eyes widened. "What about me what?"

"Why don't you pretend to be my girlfriend while you're in Dunn? We like spending time together, and it would make sense how we met. Our siblings are living together. Plus—"

"Oh, hell no," Max boomed as the back door slid

open. He stood, a tray balanced on one hand and a pair of tongs pointing at Isaac with the other. "Do *not* involve her in your bullshit."

"What's going on?" Kendall stepped onto the patio with a plate of vegetables destined for the grill.

"Nothing." Max's glare was a warning that Isaac ignored. He loved his brother, but Max was partially responsible for this fiasco.

"Meghan?" Kendall addressed her sister.

"Um…" Meghan looked from Kendall to Isaac, a question in her eyes.

"Kendall and Max know the truth," he told her, liking very much that she was willing to protect him.

"Isaac needs a girlfriend. I'm single, and I'm here. I can use my podcast to make the announcement." Meghan shrugged in no-big-deal fashion.

Well, he'd be damned. She actually sounded like she was on board. Kendall narrowed her gaze on him, and Isaac stopped grinning.

"Are you crazy? You and I admitted to the public that we were lying, and now you want to fake-date my sister?"

"No one would blink," Isaac assured her. "We could say you were protecting her, keeping her out of the limelight until she was ready."

"I'm blinking as we speak," Max grumbled while arranging meat and veggies on the flattop grill.

"*You* were the one who barged onto a television studio stage to claim Kendall like a caveman," Isaac reminded his brother.

Max and Kendall sent longing looks at each other.

God help him. How did Meghan stand being in the constant shadow of their adoration for each other?

"What's the harm?" Meghan spoke up. "It sounds fun."

"Fun?" Kendall made a choking sound in the back of her throat.

"Yes. And I don't recall asking for your approval." Meghan included Max when she added, "Either of you."

Then she shot out an arm, offering Isaac her hand. "Sign me up to be your temporary girlfriend, Isaac Dunn. I won't let you down."

He clasped her hand, amused when she gave his palm a hardy pump. Looked like his girlfriend problems were officially over. And if he was really lucky, maybe they could add some very real affection to the list. The paparazzi and fans in town would expect him and Meghan to hold hands, or kiss. Maybe a few public displays of affection were in order.

Oh, yes, she was right. This was going to be *fun.*

The next morning Meghan dressed in jeans and boots, layering a T-shirt and a hoodie since the weather was supposed to be a cool but sunny sixty-eight degrees. She jogged downstairs to find Kendall and Max snuggling by the coffeepot. She was about to make a gagging noise but was saved from it when they pulled apart.

"Morning, Meg," Max said in his low, rumbly morning voice. "Coffee?"

"Please."

"I'll grab it." Kendall tacked on a saucy wink. "Go shower. I'll be up in a second." No one missed her intentions, including Max, who offered a slightly wonky smile before jogging upstairs.

Her sister poured flavored creamer into a mug, topped it with hot coffee and handed it to her. "About your plan with Isaac—"

"My mind is made up," Meghan cut in. "I'm going to be in town, anyway. Why not have some fun while I'm here?"

"Not all of life is about having fun. I worry about you. That you're not taking this as seriously as you should."

"But *some* of life should be fun." Meghan bit her tongue before she revealed just how much her sister's words hurt. They were too close to Lane's past accusations about Meghan being irresponsible.

She had made mistakes in the past, but that didn't mean she couldn't do anything right. She had built her podcast out of nothing but a microphone and a laptop. Granted, she'd accepted Kendall's help to introduce her to Isaac and Max, but what happened from here on out would be Meghan's doing. Fake-dating Isaac would give her the experience of a lifetime and a front-row seat to the behind-the-scenes happenings of her favorite show. What more was there to consider? She was sold.

"Enjoying a dinner or two with Isaac or popping onto set a few times to meet the cast isn't exactly hard labor," Meghan continued. "Do you know how much my listeners would love some behind-the-scenes exclusives? This is good for my career, too, Ken."

"Do you know how awkward it's going to be when the two of you break up and you have to explain that to your loyal listeners?"

Hmm. Admittedly, that part of the plan gave her pause. She was less comfortable lying to her listeners.

"You haven't contended with paparazzi before. I wouldn't wish them on anyone. Not even Max's ex-wife." She was talking about Bunny, who had ended up one of Kendall's clients. She'd landed the woman a walk-on role on *Brooks Knows Best*, which Meghan was sure was more a testament to her badass sister's talents as an agent than Bunny's acting skills.

"I'm not a child anymore," Meghan reminded Kendall. "I know you're trying to protect me, but what's there to protect? Hanging out with Isaac isn't a chore. He's my favorite actor on my favorite show of all time. You like him. You trust him. Why wouldn't I say yes to him?"

"That's just it. What are you saying yes *to*?" Her sister raised one eyebrow meaningfully.

"Are you…worried Isaac will take advantage of me? Did Max say something?"

Kendall pressed her lips together.

Meghan knew it! Over dinner, Isaac and Meghan had excitedly chatted about how to announce their relationship on her podcast. He'd had great ideas. Moreover, she'd been excited by this new development. Dating him, even for pretend, sounded like a not-to-miss, once-in-a-lifetime opportunity. "It's not like he's lying to *me*."

"No, but you two are lying to everyone else."

"You mean like you and Isaac did a few months ago while you were walking around Los Angeles, hand in hand?"

Kendall's mouth dropped open into a speechless O before she snapped her teeth together and said between them, "That was different. That was for his career, and mine."

"And this is for *my* career, and Isaac's."

Kendall's lips pursed in what looked like consideration.

"Sponsors will flock to my podcast after I air the interview we recorded last night. If I follow that up with a series of interviews with cast and crew, or behind-the-scenes tidbits after I visit the set... Kendall. Can you imagine? This is the break I need. I won't have to worry about paying the bills after this. What Isaac is offering is a gift."

"You're right." Her sister sipped from her coffee mug, nodding as she swallowed. "You're right. It's a good move for you, professionally."

"Plus, I miss sex," Meghan blurted. "Not that I'm planning on having sex with Isaac."

Kendall surprised Meghan by laughing. "I can't argue with you for thinking about it. He is Max's twin, and Max is *hot*."

"Max *is* hot. Isaac is hotter in my opinion, but I'm assuming we will agree to disagree. What I meant was that I miss being *liked*. Hand-holding, even under false pretenses, would be lovely. I had fun with him at Rocky's. Talking, eating together. Laughing and sharing stories. I'm willing to be half of a couple. Even temporarily. Soon enough I'll be heading back home to North Carolina alone. I will treasure the memory of the time I stood in as the girlfriend of my celebrity crush."

Her sister put her mug down and pulled Meghan into a hug. "I'm sorry. I didn't mean to imply you were being rash."

"You didn't imply. You sort of said it outright."

Kendall held Meghan at arm's length. "I said I was *sorry.*"

"California!" came a bellow from upstairs. "Water's getting cold!"

"Go." Meghan shooed her sister off to join her very hot boyfriend in a not-so-hot shower. Then she stepped out onto the patio to finish her coffee and take in the beautiful mountains, woods and wildflowers behind the house.

She was making the right decision. She could feel it in her gut. Pretending to be Isaac's girlfriend wasn't irresponsible. If anything, it was responsible. Her ad revenue had taken a hit over the last year, and she'd begun to worry she might have to find a—*gulp*—real job. She didn't want to be tied to a desk again. She wanted to continue to grow her podcast. Isaac could help her do that.

And if, perchance, those walks while they held hands turned into snuggles or kisses or more, well... Who was Meghan to deny the natural attraction between them? She was doing this for her career more than steamy kisses under a starry night sky, but if it included both, she wouldn't argue.

She was a strong, capable, fun-loving adult. She could sign on for work and play at the same time and walk away afterward with her head held high.

Five

"Cut. Nicely done, everyone. Let's wrap for the day." Ashley stood from the director's chair and pulled off her headset. "Fantastic work, Richard."

"Thanks, Ms. Lee," answered Richard Rind, the actor who had played Isaac's character's father for a decade and was now reprising the role.

"I told you to call me Ashley."

"Got it, Ms. Lee." Richard grinned. Ashley waved him off and left Isaac and Richard on set, this one a replica of the original living room. "Nice work to you, too. I'm sure she'll tell you later."

"I appreciate that." Isaac didn't need copious compliments. One or two well-placed would suffice. And anyway, the scene he and Richard had shot as father Daniel and son Danny Brooks was one that hadn't required heavy lifting on Isaac's part. "She's right. You did a great job."

"I'm surprised. I've had quite the hiatus."

The other man's self-deprecating style was one Isaac remembered well and one of the reasons everyone was drawn to the older actor. He'd aged well, despite his stint out of the spotlight.

"I love being back." Richard lowered himself onto the striped sofa. "It was good to work with Max yesterday, too. I haven't seen you boys in way too long."

Isaac and his brother were far from "boys," but he understood how Richard saw them as kids. They'd started *Brooks Knows Best* at the tender age of five. They'd essentially "grown up" on the show, but age fifteen was a far cry from adulthood.

"Max seems happy," Richard said.

"He is. Kendall is good for him."

"Right, the agent. Your agent." Richard's eyebrows jumped. "*Not* your girlfriend, as it turned out. Where is the real one, anyhow? Don't tell me you're keeping her hidden the entire time you're on set. I want to meet her. Give her my fatherly seal of approval."

Isaac opened his mouth to offer a deflection similar to the one he'd given Ashley and Cecil and random reporters over the last few months, but then he realized he didn't have to deflect. He *did* have a girlfriend. Meghan had agreed to date him, and he was up for making their dates as real as possible.

"Not keeping her hidden." Isaac smiled. "I'm planning on bringing her by the set this week. I'll make sure it's a day you're here."

"So, she's in Dunn." Richard's gray eyebrows rose. "I can't wait to meet her. I'm happy for you."

"Richard, want to grab dinner?" Merilyn Case, who played Isaac's on-screen mom and Richard's on-screen wife, stepped onto the set. "Good job today, Isaac."

"Thanks, Mom."

Merilyn liked to be referred to as such, and with her wide waist and warm hugs, she gave off motherly vibes. Isaac's own mother was also warm and kind, but unlike Merilyn, Dani Dunn was aging as gracefully as a supermodel. She was lean and gorgeous at age fifty-eight.

"Isaac's bringing by his girlfriend." Richard shot a thumb at him as he stood from the couch.

"Oh! I have to meet her."

Isaac promised he'd bring Meghan by to meet them this week. Then he excused himself to get ready for his date. He was having dinner with her tonight.

He left work with a spring in his step. There were fans lingering on the street outside the hotel, where they'd been filming most of the interior shots, and he paused to sign autographs and take photos. Soon everyone would have what they'd been clamoring for: a peek at the mysterious girlfriend who'd stolen Isaac Dunn's heart.

After a quick stop at his apartment to change into dark pants and a button-down shirt, Isaac drove to Max's house on the mountain to pick up his stand-in girlfriend.

He wasn't what he would call rusty, but he hadn't been on a date in a while. He stuck to actresses, mostly.

Women he'd met while filming commercials or while chatting before auditions. With his recognizable face, approaching them was tricky. They were either intimidated by his quote-unquote *fame*, or they came to him with enough confidence that he'd been suspicious of their motives. Unfortunately, his suspicions had been justified, and once they'd learned he couldn't help them land a role in the latest superhero movie, they'd moved on.

Isaac had taken it in stride. He hadn't pictured having an "other half," unless he counted Max, with whom he'd shared a womb and a wildly successful career. Isaac might not have found the romantic pairing that his brother had, but he felt good about the arrangement he'd made with Meghan.

The best part about her was that she wasn't searching for more. With the show under way and his career on the upswing, he didn't have the resources to dedicate to a long-term relationship. After filming *Brooks Knows Best*, he was hoping to land a movie role worthy of his newly reclaimed fame, which would require travel, press junkets and, God willing, awards dinners.

He and Meghan had chemistry like crazy, but they would jump into this faux relationship and back out again without any pesky entanglements. That would leave plenty of room for him to focus on what mattered most: the second big break in his career, and repairing the relationship with his brother.

At Max's house, Isaac knocked on the door. Meghan answered, her honey-blond hair pulled back on one

side, her crooked smile painted red. He was too enam-
ored to speak for a handful of seconds.

"God, you're gorgeous," was what finally emerged
from his ajar mouth. She laughed, a sweet sound that
drew him in without his permission.

"Thanks." She ran a hand down a different floral-
patterned dress that ended in strappy sandals. "It's a
little cool for the evening, but I wanted to make sure
I looked nice."

"Well, you overshot nice."

One look at her, and everyone would want to know
her better. Her smile was open and friendly, her confidence understated but present. Fans would adore her,
and he'd bet his television family would welcome her
into the fray on sight.

"Hi there." Kendall appeared over Meghan's shoulder like a scolding parrot.

"Go away," Meghan said through a toothy smile.

"Where are you two off to tonight?" Max appeared
over Kendall's shoulder next, completing the Russian-
nesting-doll experience. "Not Rocky's again."

"It's none of your business where we're going,"
Meghan told them both, earning a pair of frowns. She
slipped out the door and clasped Isaac's hand, her soft,
slim fingers sending a zap of awareness up his arm.

"DeSchute's," Isaac answered. Max's mouth shrugged
in approval.

DeSchute's, a five-star restaurant in Dunn, was
perched on a hill with a stunning view of downtown.
He'd secured the best table in the house thanks to his
name and affiliation with the show.

"Does Kendall always behave like a mama bear where you're concerned?" he asked once they were settled at their table. Meghan was still gawping at the view. He could see her reflection in the window. He mentally patted himself on the back. He'd impressed her.

"She's never around to mother me." Meghan faced him. She toyed with one of the silverware pieces on the snow-white tablecloth while she talked. "I don't mind her involvement, but Max piling on is extra. Are you a masterful playboy hell-bent on ruining hearts or something?"

A loud crack of laughter escaped his throat, drawing a few curious looks from diners. "That's a new one. I'm rarely, wait, make that *never*, accused of being a playboy. Max was the one who earned the cool-rebel reputation. I'm the responsible, squeaky-clean brother."

"Or you were until you and my sinister sister lied about dating each other."

"Until. My reputation bounced back when I mentioned my girlfriend." He reached across the table and clasped her hand. "That'd be you."

"Right." Her smile brightened, thickening the air between them with sexual awareness. How were they supposed to keep their hands, or other body parts for that matter, off each other?

"I'm going to introduce you around. My director, producer and my on-screen parents are dying to meet you."

She sucked in a breath that drew his eyes to her round breasts. He inched his gaze north but her tempting red mouth was twice as distracting. "I won't let you down."

"You couldn't possibly."

A waiter delivered their wine, forcing him to release her hand when he would have been content to hold on to her the entire evening.

Dinner for Meghan was the chef's vegetarian special, which was a fancy mushroom risotto, sugar snap peas and slabs of marinated tempeh with a sticky honey-garlic sauce. The plate made Isaac's beef tartare boring by comparison. She'd fed him a bite of her risotto, the act intimate and sensual. He wondered if the food tasted good because of the prep, or because of the way she watched him with an answering hunger as he chewed.

When dessert arrived, his libido was set to stun. It was his turn to feed her, and by the time he'd spooned chocolate mousse into her mouth, he'd already decided to invite her back to his place.

During dinner he'd admired her slight cleavage and bare, delicate collarbone. Back at his apartment, he admired the way the fabric of her dress hugged every delectable curve as she took the stairs ahead of him. Her long legs and round ass wiggling in that skirt had his full attention.

He unlocked the door and let them in. She twirled around, her crooked smile as attractive without lipstick as with, and he prepared for her to leap into his arms and stick her tongue in his mouth. She walked her fingers up his shirt and cocked her head.

Come for me, beautiful.

"I was only planning on staying a few more days, but now that we've decided to be a couple, I'm thinking I should stay the month, don't you?"

He blinked, giving his brain the hard reset it so desperately needed. "Uh, yes. Yeah. Great idea."

"Great." She clasped her hands in front of her, and for the first time he picked up on a frisson of nerves.

"Drink?" He moved to the fridge. "I have beer."

"Our favorite."

He cracked the tops off a pair of beer bottles and offered her one. Standing close, he could smell the soft, clean fragrance wafting off her smooth skin. Could see the shimmer in her eyes giving her secrets away.

He wanted her, and he wasn't alone. She wanted him right back.

"We don't have to rush," he murmured, letting the comment hang between them. Her shoulders visibly relaxed when he tapped the neck of her bottle with his. "To your first acting role. Break a leg, Squire."

Six

Meghan sucked down a swallow of beer, which was refreshing after the dry red wine they'd enjoyed at dinner.

Isaac was doing his best to set her at ease, a kindness that hadn't gone unnoticed. She could kiss him for it. And she would, too. Just as soon as her tummy stopped leaping in delicious anticipation of what was to come.

Their made-for-TV romance was beginning to feel very real. She was all for having fun and squeezing every bit of pleasure from her time with him, but she also wanted to be one hundred percent present and ready. She didn't want to forget a single moment with him.

"Nice place you have here." She walked to the wide windows overlooking downtown.

"I like it." His low voice was just over her shoulder,

his warm breath on her exposed neck when he added, "The glass is tinted. No one can see you."

He smelled like leather and sandalwood with the faintest hint of citrus. As if he'd bottled the scent of his private island.

"No mountain view for you?" She turned her head, and her lips came dangerously close to colliding with his. His gaze trickled to her mouth briefly before he answered her.

"I like to be in the middle of the action. And above a deli, since I don't cook."

"Me neither. If dinner doesn't have microwave instructions, it's too much work."

"Agree one hundred percent. We're a match made in take-out heaven, Squire."

Her heart thudded when he smiled at her that way. He was so attractive. And attainable. Meeting him was a childhood fantasy come alive. Touching him, and him touching her, was an adult fantasy she hadn't known she'd been allowed to have. Needing another moment to compose herself, she reminded him of what he'd mentioned earlier.

"You mentioned coaching me for my first role?"

"I did, though I'm not sure you need it. You have the beautiful, fun and well-dressed part down."

Complimented beyond repair, she was uncharacteristically speechless.

"As long as you are comfortable holding my hand in public, and maybe a kiss or two for the fans, you have this role on lock. Just pretend you like me."

"Pretend." She emitted a delicate snort, which made her laugh behind her hand. "Isaac. I like you."

Closer to her now, he tipped his head. "I like you, too."

Pick her up off the floor, because she was pretty sure she'd fallen dead at his feet. "You do?"

"Yeah." He grinned. "That leaves one loose end. We have to make sure we're on the same page with our stories."

"Oh, right." It would make sense that they'd know about each other's pasts if they were actually dating.

"So, tell me." He paused to take a swig of beer. "About the dickheads you've dated in the past."

"One stands out above the rest," she muttered. Her dry delivery surprised Isaac. His mouth and eyebrows rose as he laughed. "What about you?"

"I've dated a lot. Not as much as you've seen on-line. A lot of times I'm photographed with cast, crew or a random barista. If she's a woman around my age, the speculation begins."

"That sucks." She couldn't imagine being romantically tied to a guy simply because he was within proximity.

"We should talk about how we met."

"At Rocky's?"

"I was referring to the fictitious way we met. I'm on record saying we fell for each other on my private island, so we should stick with that. Why were you there?"

"Easy. Kendall introduced us around the time she took you on as a client."

"When Lou retired," he said of his former agent. "Perfect timing."

"You thought it'd be a good idea for me to come with you while you prepared for your role. I offered to record a podcast to release closer to the show's release."

"Keep going," he encouraged.

Her voice rose excitedly as she continued weaving their made-up history. "While I was there, we spent more time together, *not* cooking, obviously."

"Obviously."

"Then one night on the beach while we were watching the sun set, you held my hand."

"Like this?" He clasped her fingers with his.

She swallowed around a lump in her throat, nodding since she was incapable of speaking for a handful of seconds. "Then, on the beach, while we were listening to the waves roll in, you realized you were smitten."

"Is that so?" He took her beer bottle and set it with his on the high sofa table. When he returned to stand in front of her, he was a breath away. Chest to chest, he angled his chin down to take her in as her heart raced.

Her bravado found her all at once. She met his eyes unerringly and slow-blinked. "How could you not be?"

"How, indeed." The two words preceded him leaning in, his lips hovering over hers. Nothing was between them save the exhalation she'd just released. He cupped her jaw. "Who kissed who that first time?"

"You," she breathed.

The kiss was sudden, insistent. She made a sound in the back of her throat when his fingers tunneled into her hair. He wasn't ravaging her but savoring her. The pressure he used as he slid his lips over hers suggested a hunger barely reined in. He touched his tongue to hers and her knees wobbled. But there was no way she was going to lose her balance or her mind during this exchange. She was going to savor him right back.

Fisting his shirt, she yanked him closer. He was tall, but so was she. She didn't have to strain her neck as she made out with him, which meant they could continue making out for a long, long time.

Oh, that sounds lovely.

He was all for it, flattening one palm on the back of her waist and giving her a solid yank until she was flush with his hard frame. Her breasts brushed his chest, her nipples peaking against the fabric of her bra. He grunted in the back of his throat, the sound almost helpless.

She was equally, and voluntarily, helpless. She wanted nothing more than to give in to the fire igniting between them, within them.

She hadn't had a lot of one-night stands in her past... okay, *any*. Her idea of fun had never included brief relationships. But there was something about this relationship that appealed. The guarantee of not being hurt, since she and Isaac were on the same page. He wouldn't deceive her. Their entire relationship had been constructed around deceiving everyone else. They were an innocent version of Bonnie and Clyde, in the thick of it together, until the end.

"Isaac," she whispered when he gave her space to take a breath.

"Yeah."

"Don't overthink this, but we should have sex."

The hand in her hair flinched, his fingertips imprinting her scalp. He shifted so that the stiff length of his erection was pressing into her belly. "Thinking isn't the problem. My brain's not functioning at the moment."

"I like that." Locking her arms around his neck, she continued kissing him. Her body took over, knowing exactly what she needed. This unique and beautifully erotic situation where she was liked by someone who was incredibly likable himself. Where she was being *kissed* by someone who really, *really* knew what he was doing.

His hands skated up her sides and he cupped her breasts, thumbing her nipples through her dress. Those turgid peaks jutted from behind the thin silk of her bra, greedily begging for more.

"Take it off," she whispered against his mouth.

He obeyed, unzipping the back of her dress and parting the material, his fingers drawing a line down her spine.

"What happened after I kissed you on the beach?" he asked as he slipped the top of her dress from her arms. The straps of her bra followed, and his lips landed on her naked shoulder. "Did I strip you down and take you on the sand?"

"It's your private island. You can do whatever you want."

He lifted his head, his sultry gaze drilling into her. "Can I?"

"Yes."

A primal satisfaction zipped through her, sharp and electric, when he released her dress to the floor. She gave herself over to the moment, to him. She stepped from the circle of fabric as he dipped his head and took her nipple on his tongue. Clasping the back of his head, she gasped as he cupped her sex. He applied pressure where she needed it most.

"So fucking gorgeous." His breath warmed her puckering flesh before moving to the other breast to delight her some more.

She clawed at the back of his hair, twining the longer strands in her fingers. His hands left her body long enough to slip her panties down her legs and toss them aside. He paused to place the briefest of kisses against her quivering thighs. Then he made himself at home on his knees to unbuckle the straps of her sandals.

"I can do that if you want me to."

"I've got you, Squire." He offered a wink.

Isaac Dunn was on his knees before her, his blue eyes reminding her of the Pacific waters where they'd met in her imagination. She was lost in between reality and the fantasy. Never in her wildest dreams had she thought she'd have this opportunity. He stood and scooped her into his arms, and took her to his bedroom.

"Not a beach," he said as he laid her on the bed, "but the bedspread is a shade of sandy beige."

Dusk had given away to nighttime. Moonlight painted the walls ethereal blue. He stood over her, his gaze sliding up and down her naked body. "You're killing me, Squire."

"Climb in here, and let's see if I can heal what ails you."

His grin seemed unstoppable, even as he shucked

his shirt, kicked off his pants and shoes. Before she could fully admire the swells of his biceps, the bumps of his abs or the impressive length of his cock, he was over top of her, acres of hard, hot flesh warming hers.

"Sure about this?"

She ruffled his hair and nodded. "So sure."

Satisfied by her answer, he kissed her. Then he parted her legs and slipped his fingers against her folds. His thumb found her clitoris and her hips lifted and dropped to match his rhythm.

He left her mouth to allow room for her breathy pants, teasing her breasts with swipes of his talented tongue once again. She clawed at his shoulders, pulled his hips closer with the backs of her heels. Thankfully, she didn't have to beg him. He took each of her nonverbal cues as encouragement, lined himself up with her sex and slid deep with one long, breath-stealing thrust.

Their shared moan and her reverent "Oh God" were the only sounds in the room for a beat. When she opened her eyes to find him smiling down at her, she had to smile back. Tanned skin, blue eyes, a strong nose. The perfect amount of scruff hiding a faded yet scrumptious scar. His face was stupefying, but the rest of his body was demolishing her brain cells by the thousand. He moved inside her, filling her, gently stretching her. His thrusts were slow and precise, winding her tighter and tighter.

He was *amazing*.

"Do something for me, Squire," he said with effort as he sank deeper.

"Anything." She meant it. She was lost in him. *Owned* by him.

He slid deep again, and she let out a small squeak of encouragement, her fingernails digging into his shoulders for purchase.

He brushed her nose with his. "Come for me. Say my name when you do it."

She nodded, clinging to him tighter as his next thrust liquefied her bones.

"Right...*now.*"

On his command, an orgasm rolled through her like the crashing tide on the beach in her fantasy. She said a lot of words. Praising words, swear words, unintelligible words. She was pretty sure there was an "Isaac" in there somewhere. If not, she would talk him into giving her another chance to make it up to him.

As lights burst and contracted behind her closed eyelids, she swept her hands down his sweat-slicked back, tracing the contours of his firm muscles with her fingertips. Lazily she opened her eyes to meet his pain-and-pleasure expression.

"Your turn." She flexed her inner muscles. His mouth dropped open and his eyes squeezed shut as his release shook his shoulders. He buried his face into her neck. Even so, she heard his muffled words.

He'd said her name, as well.

Seven

She didn't stay the night with Isaac. Not that she rushed off immediately following the best sex of her life. They lay in his bed for a long while, sifting through and crafting details about their imaginary island vacay. She doubted they would share most of them with the public, but she found herself enjoying having a secret. It was a bit like writing her own fairy tale, with an ending she would choose. The trick, in this case, was to lose herself in the moment and then, when the moment was over, treasure it. Which worked well for her as she was allergic to planning. Kendall was the planner and plotter. Meghan preferred to go in the direction of the wind.

Staying over would have also prompted too many questions from Kendall and Max. When Isaac had driven her home in his rented BMW, he'd taken Meghan's side and had agreed that their siblings needed to mind their own business. He hammered home the point when he mentioned Max had *zero* room to talk after impersonating Isaac not so long ago.

The next morning over pancakes—Max, unlike his twin, had no aversion to cooking and did it very well—Meghan was once again exposed to a Max-and-Kendall face suck. This time at the table.

A well-timed phone call saved her from awkwardly excusing herself. Not that Kendall and Max noticed the phone ringing. They were no longer making out, but they didn't tear their eyes from one another to acknowledge Meghan walking out of the room, either.

Outside on the patio, she curled her shoulders and braced against the chilly air. The fall day was cloudy and cool, an earlier rain having left the grass and trees both soggy and limp.

"Hi, Mom," Meghan answered after lifting the phone to her ear.

"Sorry I missed your call, sweetheart. Your father and I were at the grocery store arguing over which brand of peanut butter was best."

Meghan smiled. Her mother's exasperated tone held a note of humor. Her parents had a strong marriage, one that had grown stronger after Quinton had died. It'd always been a source of curiosity to Meghan how a shared tragedy tore some couples apart yet brought others closer.

"How is Virginia?"

"It's lovely. I'm spending a lot of time with Kendall...

when she's not spending it with Max." Which was practically never.

"New love can be irritating when you're single. At least that's what my single friends used to tell me when your father and I started dating about a hundred years ago."

"I can imagine. You and Dad still have that new-love vibe, which is thoroughly embarrassing at times," Meghan teased. A beat of silence descended, and she thought she'd better tell her mother why she'd called in the first place. "Mom, I need a favor."

"What's wrong?" The panic in her mother's voice reminded Meghan of every other phone call with her mom. Whether she'd run out of gas on the highway, or had forgotten her purse and couldn't pay for groceries, she'd phoned her mother to ask for help on more than a few occasions.

"Nothing's *wrong*. I've decided to stay in Virginia awhile longer. I don't see Kendall very often and I'm not ready to leave." Her voice climbed an octave, a sure tell that she was lying. While she wasn't *exactly* lying, she was fudging the truth a bit. Her reason for staying had less to do with vying for her sister's attention and more to do with the sexy man she'd shared a bed with for a few hours last night. "Anyway, I underpacked. Would you mind shipping me some of the clothes I keep at your house?"

Meghan spent the occasional weekend with her parents. The family home was about an hour and a half away from the farmhouse she rented. She didn't always enjoy eating dinner alone—plus, her mom was a fantastic cook and Meghan...well, *wasn't*.

"How much longer are you staying?"

"I'm not sure. Maybe a month."

"A month! Meghan, honey, what about your bills? Your job? Your responsibilities at home?"

Meghan gritted her teeth. She'd known asking her mother for this favor would include a lecture. "I pay my bills online. My job is portable, and I have a rental. The house is locked up and secure. If you could just send some clothes for me, that would be great."

"I'm sorry," her mother surprised her by saying. "I worry about you, is all. I know you're in good hands there with Kendall."

Kendall, the responsible sister. Meghan tried not to take offense but sometimes it was difficult not to read too much into her mother's comments.

"Does extending your stay have anything to do with you meeting Max's brother?"

Meghan turned to glare at the back of her sister's head. Had Kendall mentioned Meghan's date with Isaac? *To their mom?* Last night was supposed to be *way* under the parent radar.

"We adore Max," her mom continued. "When we popped out to visit a month ago, we were sold. Such a lovely man. I'm sure his brother...what's his name?"

Guess they were doing this. Meghan sighed and then answered, "Isaac."

"I'm sure if Isaac is half as nice as Max, you were ready to faint. Where did you go? Did you tell him you used to have a crush on him when you were younger? That you had a poster of him hanging over your bed? Are you two—"

"There's more to the story, Mom."

Meghan put her hand on her forehead, ignoring the sweat dampening her palm. She and Isaac would soon share their "love story" with the masses, which meant her parents would need to be fed that same story. She had little choice but to string them along as well. The truth was too bizarre, and would no doubt come with another lecture—something she'd had plenty of since she'd arrived in Dunn.

Deep breath. You can do this.

"A few months back when Max and Kendall were snowed in and shooting the commercial for Citizen watches, I was on Isaac's private island with him. It started out innocently. I was planning an exclusive behind-the-scenes podcast to help promote the show *Brooks Knows Best*. As it turns out we have a lot in common. We became friends and then, well…" She sucked in a breath and blew out the words. "Isaac is sort of… my boyfriend?"

"Your boyfriend? For how long?" Her mom gasped. "Honey, why didn't you tell me about this?"

"Isaac is a private person." That seemed true.

"Goodness, Meghan." She braced for censure, but her mom laughed before exclaiming, "How exciting!"

"What?"

"You've found someone. I'm thrilled!"

Ah, that made more sense. Her mom was glad to

have someone else involved in the handling and care of her youngest child.

"Ed! Our other daughter is in love!" her mother shouted to Meghan's dad.

Marjorie chattered to Ed about Meghan's newfound love life, pausing to ask twenty questions. Once the lightning round was finished, she promised to ship Meghan's clothes ASAP. They exchanged I-love-yous and, exhausted by the exchange, Meghan ended the call and stepped back inside.

She half expected Kendall to be at the table slurping maple syrup off Max's perfectly groomed beard, but instead she found only abandoned plates. And her sister's robe lying at the top of the staircase.

Meghan grabbed her own plate and piled it high with more pancakes, lamenting that she didn't have her own place with some privacy. Last night had been a fantastic escape. She and Isaac had had all the privacy and sensuality Meghan could hope for.

Halfway through her second sweet bite of pancakes, she was smiling at a memory of Isaac's perfect mouth and the feel of his hands on her body. Of the way he'd stroked her arm after sex and murmured in a low sensual tone about their imaginary island getaway. The way, earlier in the evening, he'd peeled her out of her dress and—

She blinked at her plate, a thought occurring. An alarming thought, which was actually a memory, or more aptly the very thing they'd forgotten.

"Oh God," she murmured as syrup dripped from her fork to the table. Isaac hadn't worn a condom. She hadn't mentioned a condom. There was no talk of protection whatsoever!

"Oh my God." She barely registered saying it aloud as she replayed the moment he'd laid her on his bed, the way she'd pulled his belt free from the belt loops. The moments leading up to the moment they…

Noooooooooooo!

Hand shaking, she dropped her fork onto her plate with a clatter. What had she done? Normally her irresponsibility extended only to overpaying for ill-advised purchases or tolerating a rude boyfriend for far longer than she should have.

The saying about putting the toothpaste back into the tube flitted through her brain followed by the one about closing the barn door after the horse had escaped.

"Thank you. Thank you for that, brain," she said under her breath. "You failed to suggest a condom last night, but you are flush with silly clichés."

She dropped her head in her hand, her vision blurring on her unfinished breakfast. What if she'd been impregnated last night? She was in no position to be a mother. She could barely care for the cactus on her windowsill at home. She forgot little things constantly—in this case a condom, which was little but forgetting it came with potentially huge ramifications.

Toothpaste and horses aside, she'd have to talk to Isaac about what happened. Had he woken this morning with similar "oh shit" clarity? There was only one way to find out.

She put one foot on the staircase, intending to ask to borrow Kendall's car, when her eyes landed on the discarded bathrobe. Best not to interrupt whatever they were in the middle of doing. Meghan was going to handle this herself...just as soon as she appropriated her sister's car keys.

Seriously, that vein is going to be the end of him, Isaac thought as he watched his producer Cecil Fowler's forehead bulge. Isaac had been late arriving to set but had made up for the lost time by nailing his lines, most on the first take. Not bad for having almost no time to practice them last night.

He grinned as he thought back on the reason why. Spending several hours with a naked, smiling Meghan Squire had been well worth being late today. He'd known she was gorgeous and talkative, but what he'd enjoyed learning was how receptive she was to him physically, and how excited she was by the idea of playing the part of his girlfriend. The women he'd dated previously had been partners in the physical sense, but never had he connected on another level. Not like he had with Meghan.

She lived in the moment and, their ruse for the public aside, she was honest and transparent. He'd been on his own for so long he'd forgotten how nice it was to have a partner who was in his corner. Who had his back. How utterly refreshing.

Cecil stopped blustering about Isaac's lateness, or as Cecil had put it, "irresponsible actions," long enough for Isaac to interrupt and change the subject. Turned out he had good news for Cecil, who had been worried about bad press surrounding the mystery woman Isaac had yet to introduce to anyone.

"Won't happen again," he told Cecil. "Good news, by the way. My girlfriend is in town and I'm finally ready for the world to meet her."

Bushy eyebrows lowered over dark eyes. "She's here? And real?"

"She's here. And real. And she's agreed to make herself a public figure for the sake of *Brooks Knows Best*. She cares so much about the show. You're going to love her." Isaac leaned in and faux-whispered, "She's also a big fan of *yours*. But don't tell her I told you that or else she'd be embarrassed."

"Oh. Well, that is good news. As long as she makes a good impression, and we don't have any negative press to contend with."

"Impossible. She's so likable not even the gossip rags will say a bad thing about her," Isaac lied. Gossip reporters had something bad to say about everything. "Not only will the public fall in love with her, you'll be doing cartwheels when you meet her. Meghan Squire is going to be great promo for the show. She's by far the best thing that ever happened to me."

He delivered the line as easily as any practiced one he'd spoken this morning. For whatever reason, part of him held on to the sentiment behind it. "Ever" might be overstating it, but she had improved his life since stepping into it.

"Squire? As in your agent?"

"My agent's sister, actually. Meghan and I—"

"Is this her?" Cecil's dark eyes zoomed over Isaac's shoulder before Isaac could roll out the rehearsed story.

Isaac turned around to find Meghan striding through the hotel's lobby toward him. He'd happened to bump into Cecil and his sour attitude outside of Ballroom B, temporarily known as the Brooks family's living room and kitchen.

Meghan, her long legs and curvy ass encased in denim, ate up the space between them with her confident stride. Even in a long-sleeved T-shirt, leather coat and sneakers, she was completely captivating.

He wasn't sure what had brought her out here with no notice, but he was damn glad to see her.

"Perfect timing, Squire." He extended an arm, folding her against him while Cecil watched their interaction skeptically. "This is my producer, Cecil Fowler. Cecil, this is Meghan Squire."

"Uh, hi. Nice to meet you." Her fake smile was obviously uncomfortable.

Maybe it was the way he'd pulled her close without warning. He loosened his hold around her shoulders and held her hand instead.

"Can we talk?" she asked.

"Always. Cecil and I were just finishing up." She didn't return his smile, frowning instead. Well. This didn't look good. One glance at his producer proved him unconvinced about how much the public would love her.

Help me out here, Squire. She wasn't her adorably charming self today, and he really needed her to be.

"As you know, Cecil has a lot of dollar bills wrapped

up in this show." Isaac gave her an intent stare, attempting to communicate that now was her time to shine. "He's been worried about your sister and me fooling the public. He implied that you and I might be faking it, too. Can you believe that?" He laughed, relieved when understanding bloomed in her bright hazel eyes. He'd gotten through to her.

"Right. Well, Mr. Fowler, that was my fault." Her lips pulled into a smile. "I wasn't ready to be in the public eye until recently." Her plastic smile remained, but it would appear authentic enough to Cecil. "My sister and Isaac's plan didn't please either Max or me, let me tell you. Especially when we both had to stay hidden while those two were photographed all over town—"

"Ohh-kay, sweetheart," Isaac added with a laugh as he hugged her close again. Too many details would make Cecil more suspicious. If that was possible. The other man seemed to be frowning with his entire body. "I wasn't going to do this here, but thanks to Cecil doubting everything, I'm going to have to convince him in another way."

Now Isaac had two pairs of eyeballs scrutinizing him. Whenever someone thought you were full of shit, doubling down was the only way to go. "You, sir," he said to Cecil, "have ruined my engagement surprise."

"Engagement?" Magically, Cecil's expression softened. Isaac took the small opening and plowed forward.

"Surprise," Isaac said to Meghan. "I was going to ask you tonight, but what's a few hours?" He dropped her hand and cupped her jaw with his palms. It wasn't hard to look into her sweet face and tell her the truth. "We're good together, Squire."

"Isaac—"

"You're the best thing that's ever happened to me. I don't want to share this life with anyone but you." He kissed her, mainly to cover their asses, but the moment his lips touched hers, he forgot their audience. He'd been craving her since he dropped her off last night. Mmm. As delicious as he remembered.

He pulled away, stunned by the vulnerability in her eyes. And the uncertainty warring with it.

"Is that a yes?" impatient Cecil asked.

Isaac's heart hit his throat. This was the first time he'd proposed—on camera or for real. As it was totally unrehearsed, he had no earthly clue what she would say.

"Y-yes."

Phew.

"Great news!" Cecil was grinning, which was a little terrifying and definitely not something Isaac was accustomed to from the brusque older man. "I'm a sucker for engagements. Fans of the show will eat this up!" He slapped Isaac hard on the arm. "Nice work, Dunn."

How about that, the man actually sounded sincere.

Meghan, having received the memo that they were improvising this scene, flashed Cecil a beaming smile and wrapped her arms around one of Isaac's. "I suspected this was coming. He's not as smooth at keeping secrets as he thinks."

Good save, Squire.

"See you around set." Cecil turned and lumbered toward the lobby.

"Sorry about that," Isaac said once he was gone. "I panicked. He wasn't buying my story and I thought we'd—"

"Isaac. I came here to talk. Find somewhere private. Right now."

But before he could lead her off to talk privately—about what, he had no idea—his on-screen parents rounded the corner and let out twin gasps of delight.

"Is this her?" Merilyn squealed.

"It has to be her," Richard sort of echoed.

"Yeah." Isaac noted his betrothed had gone rigid against him. "This is Meghan."

Eight

Whatever shock had come over her when Isaac blurted out they were engaged—seriously, *why*?—vanished into the ether when she laid eyes on... "Merilyn Case and Richard Rind."

It was impossible to conceal the awe in her voice. These two were practically rock stars—as big or a bigger part of her childhood than Isaac Dunn. The parents Brooks had been ports during the storm swirling around her after her brother had died. And here they were, in person, reaching out to shake her hand!

"It's so nice to meet you." She clasped the shorter woman's hand in both of hers. One of the women she'd looked up to her entire life, and she was shorter than Meghan. How strange. "I love you."

"Why, thank you, dear." Merilyn good-naturedly

patted Meghan's hand before addressing Isaac. "She's darling. No wonder you're nuts about her."

"Isaac mentioned he'd bring you by set and we demanded to be present when he did." Richard took her hands in his own next. "He's like a son to us."

It sank in slowly, and somewhat surreally, that Isaac had talked about her with his costars. This pretend relationship-turned-engagement was feeling more significant than before.

They excused themselves, reminding Isaac they'd meet him on set in ten minutes. That didn't give her much time to say what she needed to say. He led her to a conference room, popping the door open and flipping on the light.

"Nice work, Squire. You can add improv to the list of your talents. You caught on to exactly what I was—"

"That's not why I'm here." She didn't mean to snap, but she was running out of time, and she needed to talk to someone. She wouldn't be mentioning their accident to anyone else if she could help it.

"Okay." He folded his arms and leaned on the conference room table stacked with scripts for what she guessed was an upcoming table read. "Let's hear it."

Fiddling with the ring on her index finger, she paced to the end of the long table, and then back. How had she not settled on what to say on the way here? Once she'd arrived, there'd been no time to think about anything other than the fact that he'd been proposing to her, after which she'd met her TV in-laws.

God, this was so strange.

"Hey." Isaac caught her elbow before she made a

return trip to the opposite side of the room. "You can talk to me, Meghan. About whatever it is."

"Even if it's about last night."

His smile was gentle. He pulled her to stand between his spread legs, draping his arms around her waist. "Especially if it was about last night."

"There was…there was something missing." She raised both eyebrows, hoping her alarmed expression would clue him in.

His throat bobbed as he swallowed. "You mean emotionally," he wrongly concluded.

"No. I mean *prophylactically*."

Realization dawned on his face like a glass toppling off a high shelf. Slow to fall, and then shattering all at once. "But you— But I— You didn't say anything."

"I was too busy having orgasms." She'd been so caught up in the moment—the fantasy—that she'd neglected reality once again. How many times had her older sister told her to pull her head out of the clouds? Too many to count. "This really hot guy I've had a crush on for half my life was seducing me."

He clasped her chin, not as upset as she'd expected. "I thought you were seducing me, Squire. I was a goner."

"Really?" she whispered. His citrusy, outdoorsy scent had her fantasizing of a repeat of last night.

"Hell, yeah." He kissed her and, when he did, she forgot about the seriousness of this conversation and hauled him as close to her as possible. He spun her and pressed her back against the wall, his tongue stroking hers as his hands wandered beneath her jacket. He cradled one of her breasts as she palmed the bulge rapidly forming at the front of his jeans. In turn, he nibbled a path from her jaw to her ear. By the time she was shrugging the leather jacket from her shoulders, her back arching so she could touch as many of his hard planes at once as possible, his low, rocky voice snapped her out of a sensual fog.

"I'm starting to understand how we forgot a condom."

Yes, so was she. Maybe it had less to do with her scatterbrained personality than she'd originally suspected. They'd been seducing each other, and neither of them had paused long enough to think about the repercussions of having unprotected sex.

Slipping her hair behind her ear, he offered a steady smile. "We'll be more careful in the future. You have nothing to worry about in the STD department. I'm adamant about protecting myself. Usually. You had me in a state."

"Tell me about it." She arched one eyebrow and couldn't help smiling at the most handsome man to have ever curled her toes. "I don't want to imagine what might happen as a result of our forgetfulness."

"Then don't." He kissed her hand, his smattering of perfectly groomed scruff tickling her skin. "Most couples have to try and try *and try* to get pregnant. My cousin Rose and her husband, Jack, tried for years before they conceived. One time usually doesn't do it."

"Rose and Jack? How many times do people bring up *Titanic* to those two?"

"Often. Right before they turn into Celine Dion and belt out the movie's theme song."

She chuckled, her shoulders relaxing. How was he able to set her at ease so quickly?

"Feel better?"

Fingers resting on his chest, she soaked in his warmth. "I do."

"Good." He dropped a succinct kiss on her lips. "Bad news. I have to go back to set rather than drop to my knees and make a meal out of what's beneath these tight jeans."

Heat exploded in her chest and pooled in her belly. Then *lower*.

"That is bad news," she said, her voice raspy.

"How about tonight? I can take my time, and we won't have to rush. Or act for anyone."

"Sounds wonderful." She closed her arms around his neck, intending to kiss him one final time. Her cell phone picked that time to jangle from her purse.

"Duty calls?"

"Kendall Squire calls," she said before she answered her phone with a "Hey, sis."

"*'Hey, sis'?* Did you steal my car?"

Isaac must've overheard. His lips curved.

"Borrowed," Meghan corrected. "Calm down."

"Where did you have to go in such a hurry that you couldn't wait five minutes until I came back downstairs again?"

"Five minutes? I've stayed with you long enough to know that you and Max take longer than five minutes."

Silence. Meghan could practically hear Kendall blushing, which was oddly satisfying. Isaac covered his mouth to suppress a laugh.

"I wanted to make sure you were safe," Kendall stated, diplomatic now.

"She's safe," Isaac said into the phone, his voice hushed and accidentally seductive.

"When do you need your car back?" Meghan slid his hair away from his forehead. She liked touching him. She liked that she could.

"I don't need it right away."

"In that case, I'll keep it awhile longer. Isaac's due on set and I want to watch. We have plans later, and I'd rather not ask him to pick me up at your house if you don't need the car."

Her sister's lack of response was like a presence in the room. Meghan would bet Kendall was worried about more than her vehicle. If Ken had any idea about the Case of the Missing Condom, she'd really have something to fret about.

"Well, be safe."

Too late.

"I'll see you tonight," Kendall said.

"Do I have a curfew now?"

"Of course not," her sister huffed, sounding slightly embarrassed. "Just...tell Isaac to behave himself."

"No promises," Meghan said, her eyes on the smirking actor.

"Just...text me your whereabouts so I don't have to file a missing person's report." Kendall's exasperated sigh was interrupted by Max's low murmuring. Meghan couldn't be sure, but he sounded disapproving.

She ended the call and blew out a sigh of her own. "Will my sister ever see me as my own person?"

Isaac clasped her hand. "Don't be so hard on her. You'd miss it if she wasn't hovering. Trust me on that. Ready to go to the set?"

"If it's all right."

"I'm the star of the show. They can't tell me no."

She'd bet. She hadn't succeeded in turning him down yet.

Nine

The velvet box weighed down Isaac's pocket, practically beating like the Tell-Tale Heart. Out of last-minute options, he'd borrowed the engagement ring from the props department. It was a hunk of cubic zirconia set in platinum, but was convincing up close. It'd have to do. Might as well go big with this announcement. In a few seconds, everyone would finally meet his mystery girlfriend-turned-fiancée.

Ashley looked over at him, a question in her eyes. He nodded, the cue for her to introduce him as he'd requested before they started filming earlier.

"Before we wrap today, Isaac has a surprise for a very special audience member," she announced to the live studio audience. His fellow actors onstage sent curious glances his way. He was about to surprise everyone.

Given this was fake, he shouldn't be nervous. Becoming Meghan's fiancé was a role like any other. There were lines to recite, and he knew his motivation. But when he cleared his throat and stepped to the edge of the soundstage, the bright lights overhead, the rest of the crowd faded away.

For as long as he could remember, he'd felt like he'd been doing life alone. He was now half of a whole. He was about to make it official. Before it'd been Max who'd made up the rest of him. Now, in the eyes of the public and his coworkers, it'd be Meghan.

"Meghan, sweetheart, can you come up here?" His voice held a slight tremor. He reminded himself that the show must go on. He wasn't the only person acting in this relationship. She was, too, and he'd need to give her space to adjust and react.

As she stepped onto the stage and he took her hand, a few members of the audience whistled. A few others made high-pitched "woo" sounds.

Meghan, her smile wary, gripped his hand. He gave her a nod he hoped communicated that she could trust him, and then announced, "You've been anxious to meet the woman who stole my heart. Well, here she is."

Applause and shouts of approval infiltrated the air, from the cast and crew, and the audience. "Everyone, meet my girlfriend, Meghan Squire. Meghan, this is everyone."

More loud applause sent a rush of adrenaline through his entire body, making him feel alive. There was nothing more reliable than a studio audience. They gave the best feedback and infused the actors with the energy they needed to sell the part they were playing. He motioned for the audience to settle down, and they quieted, though excitement infused the air with a palpable buzz.

"My apologies. I misspoke," he said, turning to Meghan. "I meant to say fiancée."

Her eyes widened, her hand going to her mouth. He didn't know if she was actually shocked or doing him a solid. Either way, the audience ate up her reaction. Especially when he produced the ring from his pocket.

Only when he slid it home on her left hand did the reality of their pretend situation hit him. His palms were slick with sweat, his heart racing. As if his body had mistakenly taken this act for the real thing. But it wasn't real. Once the show had wrapped and he inevitably landed a movie deal, he and Meghan would call it done. Before she became a *Dunn*.

She glanced around at the people cheering them on, smiling their approval.

Ring snug on her finger, he leaned close and said into her ear, "They love you, Squire. Also, you'd better kiss me. They'll worry if you don't."

She didn't hesitate. She threw her arms around his neck, knocking him back onto his heels. He caught her easily, and enjoyed the soft slide of her lips gliding over his. When she pulled away, she appeared somewhat dazed, as if she'd been caught up in the moment like he had.

There, amidst the applause of the crowd that included both Ashley and Cecil, Isaac relaxed into his latest, greatest role. Fiancé to Meghan Squire, meant to boost her career, and resuscitate his. It was the perfect plan, perfectly executed, and with the perk of real-life attraction as the silver lining.

Through a frozen smile, Meghan asked, "Now what?"

"Now you wave," he answered, lifting his hand to do the same. "And enjoy your newfound fame."

After the proposal on set, Meghan and Isaac were waylaid by well-wishes from the cast and crew present. It seemed everyone wanted to congratulate them, and why wouldn't they? They adored him and, like she'd told him before, people were rooting for him.

"We have a hashtag," she said from her chair across from his at the deli beneath his apartment. Her cell phone screen aglow, she showed him their new nickname.

"Squnn?" Sandwich in his grip, he screwed his mouth to one side.

She wrinkled her nose. "Not very flattering, is it?"

"Best not to become flattered by anything you read," he warned after taking a bite of his turkey Reuben. "For every handful of positive, gushy comments, you'll find one that is pure vitriol straight from hell."

"Yikes." She slid her phone into her purse. Perhaps that was enough internet use for the day. "I've never received this much attention, but I have heard from trolls with something negative to say about my podcast. Those types of comments hurt, but I didn't let it stop me."

"Well, good for you for not quitting. They can burrow under your skin if you let them. You have to remember that you're valuable and worthy of doing what you love."

It wasn't the first time someone had rallied around her chosen profession, but Isaac's approval felt the sincerest. He was legitimately famous, to the point of being recognized on the street. He'd been at the top and then close to bottom and was on the way up again. A vote of confidence from a man with his experience meant the world to her.

She thanked him, and he explained that she had nothing to thank him for, that they were in this together, and again, she felt a part of something bigger than herself.

"I was thinking." He dusted his hands on his jeans. "You should move in with me while you're here. We're crazy in love and engaged. Wouldn't make any sense for you to stay with Max and Kendall."

It was a valid point. What real couple would remain apart after a romantic and very public proposal?

"Plus, you won't have to listen to Max and Kendall having sex at all hours of the day and night."

She laughed so hard she made a soft snorting sound. His sandwich finished, he leaned over the table for two and lowered his voice, even though they were in a private, empty corner of the deli. "Wouldn't you rather listen to you and me do it?"

Her cheeks warmed at the thought of more time in bed together. Of course she'd sleep with him again. No way would she miss that opportunity. Them sharing an apartment would also mean she wouldn't have to go back to her sister's cabin afterward.

"You're sure?"

"In for a penny, in for a pound." He tossed his balled-up napkin on the table. "We're doing this one way, Squire."

"All the way?" she guessed.

"My way. I have everything under control this time around. The show's reboot is my second chance. You're an integral part of my comeback."

She smiled, liking being included in his dreams and goals. He didn't treat her like she was a problem or like she was screwing things up. He trusted her.

She trusted him, too.

Her prayers that Max and Kendall would be mid-nookie by the time she arrived at their house had gone unanswered.

Isaac had followed Meghan so that she could drop off Kendall's car and then return to his apartment with him. Their plan had been solid, but it hadn't worked out. Rather than slip in and pack a suitcase, and then slip out undetected, she was packing said suitcase with Kendall standing sentinel.

"Mom's shipping me clothes. Can you bring them to Isaac's place when they arrive?" It was a desperate attempt to deflect from the obvious topic, but worth a shot.

"It's not a good idea, Meg," her sister said for the third time.

"We're engaged, Ken." She wiggled her bejeweled ring finger for effect. "And before you warn me, I know this is for *funsies*, not real life. This has to look legit. How long do you think it'll be before Mom calls?"

Lying to her parents about the relationship-turned-engagement was another part Meghan wasn't looking forward to. At least she could do it over the phone instead of in person.

"You'd better call her before she calls you." Kendall leaned one slender hip against the bureau. She'd moved here from California, but still dressed the part. High-end fashion from head to toe, she wore brand-name blue jeans and a slouchy sweater. Her hair was twisted into a glamorous but meant to look sloppy topknot. She shook her head, sending wide gold hoop earrings waggling. "Why wasn't dating him enough?"

Meghan supposed she could blame Isaac for springing an engagement on her, but she'd had enough of Kendall treating her like a daughter instead of a sister.

"Isaac and I are engaged, and we are moving in together. End of the story." Despite the clipped statement, Meghan delivered the news gently, not wanting to hurt her older sister's feelings. Isaac had said she'd miss it if Kendall didn't hover, and since Quinton wasn't around to hover, Meghan knew that was true. "It'd be nice if you were supportive instead of judgmental. I am an adult."

Kendall's lips pursed and Meghan could guess what was going through her sister's head. *An adult who rarely plans ahead, barely has enough money to rent a house and is lost in a fantasy with an actor she's been in love with since she was a tween.*

"Okay," Kendall said instead of any of that.

"Okay?"

Kendall came out of her lean and stuffed her hands in her pockets. She shrugged one shoulder. "I'll stop lecturing you. But you have to promise to let me know if you need me. I've been through this once—pretending to be in a relationship that wasn't real. With the same man you're pretending with, I might add."

"Yes, but you were also afraid you'd lost Max. I don't have the love of my life on the line. Well, only a fake one."

There would be no happily-ever-after ending for Meghan and Isaac, not that she wouldn't be "happy" when this was over. She would appreciate the time they'd spent together. Plus, she'd be too busy with her wildly successful podcast to foster a long-distance relationship if they did have second thoughts about breaking up.

She had big plans after leaving Dunn. She was going to be flush with sponsorships and famous guests and ad money. She'd probably have to hire a staff to help her edit or handle her online marketing. And, oh! Don't forget advertising. Yes, she'd have her hands full once this fake-fiancée business had concluded.

She snapped out of her musings to notice she was halfway between the dresser and bed, her hands full of underwear.

"I need to invest in sexier undergarments." She shook a handful of Hanes cotton. "These are boring."

"So, you *are* planning on sleeping with him."

"Yes. Again."

"Again?"

"Again." She waggled her eyebrows.

"Well…" Kendall tipped her head to one side, her mouth shifting into a conspiratorial tilt. "He is cute."

"No." Meghan stuffed the rest of her clothes into her suitcase. "Kittens are cute. Isaac is *hot*."

How long did it take to pack a bag?

Isaac glanced at the top of the stairs, but there wasn't a sign of Meghan yet. When they'd walked through the front door, she had announced she wasn't going to be staying here any longer before saying hello. Kendall's mouth had flattened, her accusing glare on Isaac, before following Meghan upstairs. Protective-older-sister mode was dialed up to ten.

Max and Isaac had cracked open a couple of beers and settled in at the kitchen table, where they still sat. Max's beer was empty, Isaac's warming in front of him with only one sip missing. Max hadn't spoken in a long while. Finally, he did, and said not a single word Isaac had been expecting.

"You can trust her. Meghan."

"I know."

Blue eyes matching his own swept to him. "Can she trust you?"

Max, the consummate older brother, was back to bossing Isaac around like he didn't have two brain cells to rub together. They were the same damn age, separated by mere seconds. Frustrated, Isaac opted for sarcasm.

"Nope. She can't trust me. I'm going to break up with her publicly, ruining her hard-won reputation and mine and then lurk around my evil castle on the hilltop where I'll live out my remaining days in dark solitude."

"Don't be a smart-ass."

"Don't treat me like I can't function without you." Isaac reclaimed his beer, catching Max's expression. A dab of hurt seeped in before vanishing altogether. "Meghan can function on her own, too."

When they were kids, Isaac had felt like he hadn't been able to function without Max. Conversely, Max had had no problem functioning without Isaac. It hurt, to need Max more than Max needed him. For a long while, Max hadn't needed anyone. For the first time, Isaac was independent from his brother but not miserable about it. He could thank Meghan for that. Being intertwined with her was helping him not to feel so alone.

"Our world of make-believe is new to her. She is a massive fan of the show. Of us. She made a career out of talking about *Brooks Knows Best*. Now you're sliding a ring on her finger and proposing. She's moving in with you. How sure are you that she understands what's real and what's not? You're an actor. You *know* how to separate fact from fiction."

Isaac hadn't thought of it in that exact way, but he and Meghan had talked a lot about fact and fiction. She was excited about this. Sure, the engagement had been a surprise, but she'd rolled with it. "Meghan can handle a little pretending."

"You sleep with her yet?"

"None of your business."

"A physical relationship is a fact, brother," Max's do-as-I-say-not-as-I-do speech continued. "If she is comfortable in your bed and kissing you in public and telling the press how over the moon you are for each other, how can you be sure she doesn't have the wrong idea?"

"Believe it or not, Max, this is well-traveled territory. She and I have the same goals. To boost our careers and enjoy the time we spend together. We have a plan. We don't need your input. As I recall, you never asked for mine when Kendall ended up snowed in here with you, or when you impersonated me in that watch commercial."

Max's mouth flattened. His expression didn't quite reach abashed, but he didn't say any more on the topic, either. His was the ultimate pot-calling-the-kettle-black situation. Kendall and Max had stirred up plenty of trouble and had involved Isaac when he'd been minding his own business on his private island.

"Ready!" Meghan called, jogging down the stairs with packed bags.

Finally. He wondered if she was as ready to escape Kendall's scrutiny as he was Max's.

Ten

Meghan carried her purse while Isaac toted the rest of her luggage into his upstairs apartment. At the threshold of his bedroom, he paused.

"Are you okay staying in here with me?"

She nodded, feeling oddly shy.

He settled her bags next to the bed and she dropped her purse onto the dresser. An awkward moment descended as they stood in silence.

It hadn't occurred to her until just now that moving in with Isaac would mean sharing a bedroom during other times, not just when they were naked together. As intimate as sex had been, sleeping next to him or sharing morning coffee seemed more so.

"What do you want to do first?" he asked, crossing his arms. He'd shoved his shirtsleeves up, revealing sinewy forearms. His slow grin was contagious and soon she was smiling back at him.

"Is this shortsighted?" she asked, hating that she wasn't sure. Shortsighted might as well be her middle name.

"This as in…" He gestured around the room. *"This?"*

"We know what we're doing, right?"

"Absolutely," he answered with enough certainty that she believed him. "We're going to hang out for the next month. Here, around town and on set. When filming is done, we'll act as if we're maintaining a long-term relationship. In a few months—or hell, weeks—fans will lose interest. We'll fizzle out naturally."

"That sounds doable." His confidence set her at ease. He understood the world of fame better than she did. Plus, Kendall and Max knew how to circumvent the public, or involve them, when necessary. "Just making sure I'm not being rash."

"Are you often rash?" He stroked her arm with his fingertips, captured her hand in his and slid their fingers together.

"I have been known to make a foolish decision here and there. Did I tell you about my time-share in Florida?"

"Say it isn't so." His tone was light, and a soft chuckle followed. Nothing like the way Kendall had reacted when she'd learned Meghan had sunk her savings into the bad investment. Kendall had used that same scolding older-sister tone from earlier. The one that painted Meghan as the problematic Squire.

"It's so. If I manage to book outside of the company's blackout dates, you can come visit."

"Nah. I'll take you out to Belle Island instead."

Her breath caught as she imagined visiting his private island, the one she'd pictured over and over. How fun would that be? But then she figured he hadn't been serious about the offer. His plan hadn't included them having an actual long-distance relationship, or vacationing together. Not that she was anywhere near ready for a relationship of the magnitude of their pretend one. Being engaged for real would mean choosing where they would live permanently. How would that work with Isaac on one coast and her on the other?

She shook off the thought. She was getting ahead of herself. There was no future that included them dating beyond their temporary status. She glanced down at her ring. "Does it have a backstory I should know about? Was it your grandmother's? A family heirloom?"

"Grandmother's ring is in Max's possession." He kissed her hand. She couldn't tear her eyes off him when he'd been on her television screen years ago, or when he'd been on set earlier today. And now, a breath away from her, not staring at him became equally impossible. He brushed the chunky teardrop diamond with his thumb. "This one is a fake."

"Really?" It didn't look fake. The stone—or whatever it was—glinted in the dim light, twinkling like an actual diamond.

"I lifted it from the props room."

"You didn't!"

"Did."

"Will you get in trouble?"

He shook his head. "I doubt it. They probably won't notice it's gone."

The faux diamond twinkled when she wiggled her fingers. "This sounded like fun at first. Just a white lie to save you from bad publicity and draw in the good. Are we lying to ourselves as well as everyone else?"

"No. We're giving the public the version of the truth they want. Plus, we're not lying to each other. That's what matters. Your sister and my brother are afraid we're going to hurt each other, but you and I have an agreement. We're not going to do that."

"We won't." Not only could he trust her, she could trust herself. "We have the widest, most open eyes imaginable. We're better off than most couples. We know what's beneath the attraction."

She rested her palm over his thumping heart. He closed his hand over hers and his pupils darkened, eating up the blue surrounding them.

"Which means we are free to focus on the attraction part."

"Yes. That's exactly what it means." She plucked a button free on his shirt, then another. Once his shirt was open, she ran her hand over his tanned skin, dark chest hair and along the bumps of his taut abs. Her entire body tightened when his did, their shared desire saturating the scant space between them.

He whispered the words "My turn" and then pulled her shirt over her head.

There was still a part of her that couldn't believe she was sleeping with, and now living with Isaac Dunn. *And* he was kissing her. Again! It was her teenage dream come true, but where they were headed was for adult eyes only. For *his* eyes only.

He took off her bra, sliding the straps from her shoulders slowly. She closed her eyes and indulged in the feel of his lips on hers. On the way he tugged and pulled, alternating from firm pressure to gentle sips.

He kissed her neck, along her collarbone and then down to her breasts, paying particular attention to her sensitive nipples. For long, sumptuous minutes, he drove her wild above the waist.

Anxious and impatient, she clawed his head and begged him to let her get naked. He grinned, his mouth damp, his eyelids drooped seductively. "Talked me into it, Squire."

She stripped her jeans from her legs, and he followed suit. Naked, they fell into bed, him on top, her legs parting naturally to accommodate him. When she lifted her legs to wrap them around his waist, she noticed again how seamlessly they fit together.

He didn't rush to enter her, instead kissing her mouth some more. Like he was memorizing her flavor. She lingered in the moment, allowing him to lead while she reciprocated. He dove in with his tongue before retreating, repeating the pattern until she was pulling his hair and practically gasping for air.

He peppered soft kisses along her jaw. He nibbled on her ear, her neck. He kept his hands busy, sliding them down to cradle her breasts, gliding over her belly and then cupping her sex. His talented fingers danced intimately along her seam as she squirmed in delicious agony. There was only one way to satisfy the ache that had built inside her. She was done waiting.

Cupping his erection, she stroked his shaft until he was hard and heavy in her palm. He groaned as he devoured her mouth and she arched closer, needing him to fill her to the brim.

He glided the head of his cock through her silken folds, his tongue tangling with hers while she urged him forward.

Don't stop. Don't stop. Don't stop.

But he did stop.

He blinked at her, both dazed and beautiful. His hair was a disaster from her wandering fingers, his wicked smile obliterating half her brain cells.

Leaning close, his lips brushed hers when he said, "We're doing it again."

"I know," she purred. "We're damn good at it."

He laughed, that wonderful sound rolling over her. "Can't argue with you there, but I'm talking about forgetting protection."

"Oh. Oh my God." She slapped her hand to her forehead. "I swear I don't do this on a regular basis. It's just with you…" She trailed off, unsure how to finish that sentence.

"I know the feeling." Off the bed now, he riffled through his nightstand and came out with a foil packet. Rolling on the condom, he said, "You muddle my head, Squire. I think I'm starting to like it."

Sheathed and ready, Isaac approached the bed where a gorgeous blonde was opening her arms to him. He appreciated the trust that had grown between them, but he enjoyed their potent sexual chemistry more.

She accepted him against her, digging her heels into his ass, urging him forward. His elbows resting on the bed, he toyed with the wavy strands of her silken hair, marveling at the way her perfect mouth parted to let out a breathy sigh. This was his favorite look on her—beneath him, with that little pleat separating her fair eyebrows.

Long, lush lashes shadowed her high cheekbones, her eye makeup thick and dark on the lid and sparkly and soft above. He was fascinated by her. Like he'd found a rare creature in the most unlikely of places.

She was also the ultimate safe space. He knew what came next in their timeline. There was a plan with an end date. And while the idea of ending wasn't what he wanted to focus on, there was comfort in knowing they wouldn't have a messy split. No one's heart would be broken. Their attachment was temporary with a clearly marked exit sign at the end. He'd walk away whole and so would she. Happily-ever-after looked different for them, but that didn't mean they couldn't enjoy the ride.

He found the pulsing heart of her deep within and thrust forward. Her mouth opened into an O of pleasure, her arms and legs tightening around him. Sex with her was worth whatever bumps in the road they encountered. Connecting was difficult in the most ideal situations. He'd been walking around in pieces for so long he'd forgotten what it was like to be held together by someone else.

He wasn't on the same trajectory as his older brother.

He wasn't planning on settling down with a marriage and kids in his future. He had to be available for what came next. Which could be an extensive filming schedule, or relocating to another state or country. Maybe later, after he'd landed that coveted second big break, he'd consider settling down. His career was number one right now. Acting was the true glue holding him together—the one thing he could count on. He'd been holding out for this dream for so long he couldn't abandon it now.

Acting energized him in the morning and kept him from falling asleep right away at night. He was on fire with a love for the set, and Meghan was paving the way for him to succeed. He was exceedingly grateful for her, and intended to show her just how much.

Her fingertips spearing upward into his hair, she yanked, her eyebrows pinched, her moans breathy. She murmured his name, followed by, "Please," and hell, who was he to deny her what she needed?

He liked nothing more than winding her tight and watching her go over. That first time they'd had sex he'd been lost in her. No wonder they'd forgotten the damn condom. He'd managed to remember this time, and now there was no reason to interrupt the flow. He was looking forward to her release as much as his own.

He could let go with her. Not only physically, but emotionally. He could let the elusive feeling of wholeness take over and fill his chest to capacity. He'd had the strange and disconcerting worry the feeling would never return. But in this private space with Meghan in his bed, he'd found it. The gift he never would have asked for, yet she gave to him freely.

He sank into her solace once again. Her eyes opened, bathing them in their golden glow. He let loose, pouring everything he felt into her as he plunged deep again.

He moved her an inch up the bed, thrust again and shoved her higher. Her focus wavered, her eyes glazing over with undiluted satisfaction. At her whispered, "Please," he pumped faster, harder. She clamped down on him with those glorious inner muscles and came. Her neck arched as her nails scratched down his back.

"Isaac. *God*." The word faded on a wheeze when the orgasm stole her breath. When she clutched again, lifting her hips to greet him, he followed.

His release rocketed through him, taking with it his earlier thoughts. What had been sharp and clear blurred at the edges. He pressed his lips to her ear and said, "Meghan."

"I'm here. I'm here."

"I know." Eyes closed, he shuddered against her, and sank into the welcome abyss.

Eleven

Max rolled his script in between his hands as he leaned back on two legs of the wooden chair at the Brooks family dining room table. They were taking five, or as Ashley had said, "however long Bella needs to relieve herself," before they resumed filming the scene. Max's walk-on role as the neighbor with a rambunctious Saint Bernard, aka Bella, was popping up again in episode four.

"You're a natural. You should get a dog," Isaac told his brother before cracking open a can of sparkling water. Raspberry in this case—not his favorite, but the only flavor on the food cart.

"Why would I need a dog?"

"Companionship for the hikes you take into the woods."

"I have Kendall. Not that she's much of a hiker. But she's getting there. At least she has decent shoes now that she lives with me."

Isaac chuckled. He didn't necessarily consider Kendall high-maintenance, but neither was she as laid-back as Meghan.

"Hate to say this," Max started, making Isaac tense in anticipation. "But I like being back on set."

"Why do you hate to say it? Because you resisted it with everything inside of you for so long?"

"Something like that," his brother admitted. "It might not be my thing, but it's been fun to moonlight as a famous person."

"Dude, you have a town named after you. You're a famous person *always*." Isaac was having a hell of a good time performing with his brother. They were together again, slipping back into the rhythm they'd had on set as kids, only this time around they were playing two different characters. "It's too bad we were never in the same scenes together before. You might have stuck it out in this business if you'd enjoyed yourself more."

"I still would have left."

"Ouch."

"It's nothing personal." Max leaned forward and whacked Isaac in the leg with the rolled script. "I'm sorry I was a bear about it before. Reuniting with everyone has been...nice."

Max wasn't known for his compliments or grand statements. *Or* apologizing. Isaac clutched his chest and pretended to have a heart attack. "Did you say you were sorry?"

Max ignored Isaac's theatrics, tipping his head in the direction of the living room set where Meghan was chatting with Merilyn, her hands waving animatedly in front of her while she spoke. "How's everything going?"

It was fucking *great*.

They'd gone out to pick up coffee every morning, and then she'd walk with him to M Hotel, where the show was filming. Afterward, she'd either stick around like she had today, or head back to the apartment to work on her podcast, or her website, or one of the other million things she did. She was a hard worker, and ambitious. He didn't understand why she referred to herself as flighty or rash. She'd accomplished more than most entrepreneurs he knew.

He planned on taking her out for dinner tonight. Sex had been a daily occurrence, twice on some days, *three times* today if he could squeeze in a break and sneak her into an empty conference room. Here was hoping Bella needed an extra lap around the park.

"I take it by your dopey grin, it's good," Max said, his smile knowing.

"It's great, man. She's…great." A lame adjective, but he wasn't about to admit to his brother how she made him feel alive again, or that her nipples were the perfect rosy shade of pink, the likes of which he'd never seen before. And he definitely couldn't share that they'd been making love on the closest piece of furniture because they were too impatient to go to the bedroom first. "I don't know what you or Kendall were so worried about."

"Kendall means well," Max said. "They lost a lot when they lost their brother, you know?"

"Their brother," Isaac blurted before realizing he *didn't know* she'd had a brother, let alone that he'd passed away.

Max's eyebrows bent in sympathy. "She didn't tell you?"

"No, ah, I guess it didn't come up."

"Might want to debrief each other on the basics." His brother turned to look over his shoulder to where Meghan was hugging Ashley. "She's in tight with your crowd, looks like."

"Yeah. She fits in wherever she is," Isaac muttered, but he was still stuck on the fact that his temporary fiancée hadn't shared her brother's death with him. They'd mentioned their families on several occasions. It should have come up. Did she not trust him?

Meghan bopped over to where they were sitting, her red lips parting in a smile. "Looking good out there today, Max. Is acting like riding a bike? It all comes back to you when you're in the moment?"

"It's more like riding a camel. It's uncomfortable and you look awkward doing it, but it's still fun."

She giggled, her smile holding when she faced Isaac. "I'm going to head over to Luxury Bean. Kendall wants to go shopping and grab lunch."

"I'll walk you."

"Won't you be late for your scene?"

"I'll cover for him," Max said.

Well. Isaac would be damned. Not only was his twin brother stepping in, but also stepping *up* for him.

"Thanks, man," Isaac told him.

Max shrugged.

His hand in Meghan's, Isaac weaved through the set toward the hotel exit. He wanted to ask her about her brother but wasn't sure the best way to bring it up.

"Press is thicker than last week," he said instead. "We might be stopped today."

"What should I do?" Her fingers tightened around his.

"Wave and smile. Don't feel pressured to answer their questions. I'll be asked about us during more formal interviews, so I can field the big stuff."

He paused before they stepped outside. He needed to know the details of her past so he could support her through this fake relationship. He also needed to be sure he wasn't blindsided by the press. If anyone other than Max had brought up her brother's passing, they would have found it bizarre if Isaac didn't know. That could have blown their cover wide open.

He faced her. "If there's anything in your past or about your family I should know, you should tell me."

He'd half expected her to avoid mentioning what he was fishing for, but she nodded matter-of-factly instead. "You mean Quinton."

"Max mentioned you and Kendall had a brother."

"He was twenty when he died." She offered a sad smile. "I was eleven. Your show helped me through a rough, sad time in my life."

"I'm sorry. You don't have to go into details." He hazarded a glance around the lobby, but no one was within earshot of them.

"Thank you. Losing him hurt, and probably always will. But I know he's never far. I can feel him around."

If Isaac lost Max, as in *permanently*, he'd dry up and crumble into a pile of dust. And yet Meghan, with her strength, beauty and resolve had walked through fire and come out the other side better for it.

"You're remarkable, did you know that?"

She laughed as if amused. "I try to live in the present. Only this moment is real."

Through the front door entered a slobbery Saint Bernard and her owner/handler. "All set!" the woman announced as she walked past them.

"Go." Meghan nudged him. "I'll be fine out there. If anyone jumps me on the way to the coffee shop, I'll deflect with a joke and shoot them a dazzling smile."

She shot Isaac one such dazzling smile. He clasped her waist and kissed her, too brief for his taste, but better than nothing. "If you're sure."

"I've got this, Dunn." She blew him a kiss as she backed toward the lobby exit. He admired the cute skip in her step as much as her long legs in dark tights ending in tall shoes. Her chocolate brown dress and leather coat made her look like a star herself. He couldn't have picked anyone better for their shared mission.

Whistling, he strode back to the set, encountering Ashley on the way. The director cocked her head, her expression curious. "Happy about something, Isaac?"

"About lots of things."

Everything, in fact. How rare.

Meghan hefted the heavy box up the rest of the stairs, regretting telling Deli Dave (as she'd come to nickname the owner) that she didn't need his help. Kendall was behind her, loaded down with a bag from the deli—a turkey and Swiss for her and a deluxe veggie for Meghan—as well as the shopping bags from their mini excursion today.

Inside Isaac's apartment, Kendall set their lunch on the kitchen counter. "Wow. Nice place you got here."

"You haven't seen your boyfriend's brother's place yet?" Meghan dropped the box on the couch and tore the tape. "Then again, you rarely leave your sex nest."

"You can't be jealous of Max and me now that you're bopping your teenage crush in a fancy mansion-like apartment."

Kendall unwrapped her sandwich and took a bite as Meghan pawed through the clothes her mom sent.

"Oh God." She held up one of the sparkly tops.

"What?" Kendall asked around a bite.

"Mom knows I'm having sex with Isaac." She tossed the top aside and held up a formfitting black dress. "Look at this tight little number."

"*I* didn't tell her," Kendall said. "Come and eat. I've finally stolen away from my, what did you call it, sex nest?"

"Do you prefer love cave?"

"Ew!" Kendall wrinkled her nose. "No, I do *not*."

Halfway through their sandwiches, Meghan's phone trilled, the sound signifying a new business email. She opened the app and gawped as she read.

Holy crap.

Kendall, who'd been watching her closely, put her sandwich down. "What is it?"

"Fawn Beauty wants to sponsor my podcast."

"Impressive. Fawn Beauty is a big name."

Huge. This was the miracle Meghan had been hoping for. She'd recently updated her rates for advertising on her podcast. Now Bethany at Fawn Beauty wanted a Tier 3 advertising package! Tier 3 was her most expensive tier, which was a blessing since Meghan had charged the last three months' rent on her credit card. She was running out of time, and nearing her credit limit.

Kendall's satisfied smile remained as she bit into her sandwich. Meghan pursed her lips, narrowing her eyes in suspicion.

"Why aren't you surprised?"

"I know how good your podcast is. Plus, you are engaged to Isaac Dunn, which was apt to draw some attention."

"Kendall," Meghan warned.

"Fine! I put feelers out. I wanted to help—"

"No! No helping!" Meghan's shoulders sagged. She'd wanted to succeed on her own. Prove once and for all that she could handle her own problems. Her own *life*. "I'm not your client."

"No, but you are my sister. I love you. And I have connections." Kendall tapped her breastbone. "Use me."

Meghan frowned at her lunch, her appetite gone. Fawn Beauty's attention had come thanks to Kendall's influence, not Meghan's reputation.

"You practically begged me to introduce you to Max and Isaac so you could interview them and your podcast would gain more traction. What's wrong with greasing the wheels a bit with the company owners I know?"

"What's *wrong* is that the interview wasn't about money. Not directly," she added, because obviously having famous guests would mean bigger sponsors for her show.

"You are doing a long-running series on *Brooks Knows Best*. Isaac, my client, stands to gain from it, and he pays me to manage his career," Kendall defended. "The lines are a little blurry."

Okay, so her sister was making a teeny-weeny smidge of a point.

"All I did was suggest your podcast as a good fit for women ages twenty-one to forty-five. They did the rest." Kendall held up her hands in don't-shoot-the-messenger style.

"Thank you." Meghan tried to stymie her begrudging tone but wasn't totally successful. "Next time, ask me."

"You would have said no."

"You don't know that."

"*Fine.* I'll ask next time."

Satisfied, Meghan resumed eating. Kendall waited until Meghan's mouth was full to add, "But you still would have said no."

Twelve

Isaac wasn't the kind of guy to walk around feeling blessed or spouting cheesy clichés when someone asked how he was doing. But when Helen at Luxury Bean asked how his day was going, he heard himself answer, "Never been better." That was an improvement from the answer he'd given the boom mic guy, which was, "Too blessed to be stressed."

Yikes.

He was whistling as he walked up the stairs to his apartment while carrying two cups of coffee. One was Meghan's French roast with whipped cream on top, the other his double espresso. He'd finished filming a night shoot, sneaking in a catnap around four in the morning. He should be exhausted but was buzzing from an earlier espresso as well as harnessed excitement. Now at eight o'clock, he planned on waking Meghan with a coffee and morning sex, or maybe the other way around depending on her level of alertness.

Life was going according to plan, which was a rarity for him. He'd never known it was possible for a splintered past to heal, but wholeness was peeking around the corner at him. What he had with Meghan was part of it. The show, a bigger part. His brother, another piece of the puzzle. Kendall had even texted to say she was reaching out to inquire about auditions for potential blockbuster movies, which would send Isaac's career soaring.

Whistling, he opened his apartment door. Meghan was seated behind her laptop, headphones on and microphones hot. Richard and Merilyn were across the table from her, and each offered a silent wave.

Meghan had been midsentence but recovered easily, giving him a smile. "That whistling you just heard belongs to none other than my famous fiancé," she announced into the mic. "And, oh, what's this? He brought me a coffee. Is it any wonder why I love him?"

His steps faltered at the pronouncement, so unaccustomed to hearing a woman profess her love for him. Those three words could threaten his stability. If his and Meghan's relationship exited fake territory, it would be harder for him to keep the balls he was juggling in the air.

He couldn't deny a part of him longed to hear those words, but he also couldn't afford to give them any real weight in his life. Not while everything was so tenuous.

Richard and Merilyn were both smiling at him like

doting parents and Isaac reminded himself not to jump to conclusions. This was the facade, and Meghan was playacting like he'd asked her to from the beginning. Nothing had changed between them, and he didn't have anything to worry about. His house of cards still stood.

Bending to kiss Meghan's cheek, Isaac leaned close to her microphone and said, "I'm a catch, what can I say?"

He quietly vacated the kitchen area for the en suite off the master bedroom. Confident he wouldn't make too much noise since the bedroom was far enough away from the microphones, he finished his coffee, took a much-needed shower and brushed his teeth. By the time he'd dressed, Meghan's tone had shifted from live-podcast mode to casual. After three weeks of living together, he could tell the difference between the two.

Despite his crazy schedule and hers, they managed to make time for each other. They had sex regularly, more every other day than every day. Oddly enough he was almost as content with curling her against him on the sofa while watching movies as he was turning her inside out beneath the covers.

She was an ideal partner. She'd transitioned into the role of his fiancée seamlessly, never asked too much of him and didn't complain about his hours. If all relationships were this simple, he would have been married by now.

The idea of forever gummed up the works. Arguments held more weight when you knew you'd be having them until death-do-you-part. The time and energy they required would mean less time and energy for other important aspects of life, like a career revival in his case.

Her mentioning she loved him had sent a jolt through him that was more panic than longing. *Love* was the biggest four-letter word there was and required more than he had to give at the moment. But that'd been Meghan's way of selling the fantasy to the public. Her admission was similar to him reciting lines from a script.

He exited the bedroom in time to say goodbye to his on-screen parents. He shook Richard's hand and pulled Merilyn close for a hug, promising to see them on set later. They mentioned what an amazing interviewer Meghan was, and Isaac was surprised to see her cheeks grow warm from the flattery.

"Don't be shy about how talented you are," he told her as he shut the front door. "Surely you're not intimidated by them. They're the sweetest."

"They are. I'm a little starstruck around them. I can't help it."

"Ah, I remember when you used to feel that way about me." He wrapped his arms around her waist. "Miss me?"

She answered with a soft kiss. "Thank you for the coffee."

"You're welcome." An idea that'd been forming over the last week or so had gelled in his mind today. The next step in the plan had come along naturally. He had no idea how she'd react until he asked. Here went nothing. "So, we're almost done filming. Another week or two and Ashley will call a wrap."

"That went fast." Her eyebrows rose, but her expression gave nothing away. Did it feel too soon or like a long time coming? Was she ready to go home and leave this experience behind?

He cleared his throat and powered through. "Remember how, when we made this agreement, we decided to part ways once I went back to LA? I told you I'd handle the press and we'd allow them to believe we were carrying on long-distance until the attention surrounding us naturally fizzled out?"

Her eyes narrowed. "Mmm-hmm."

"I want you to come to California with me instead. Ending what we have in a few weeks' time is abrupt. It'll look bad, for one, and two—" he gripped her hips and pulled her close "—I'm not done with you yet, Squire."

Heat bloomed in her eyes but shuttered a second later. She pushed against his chest. "Isaac…"

"Just until the show actually airs," he said before she could argue. "Not that I'm superstitious, but it seems like bad luck to stop while things are going well, don't you think?"

"Until the show airs? In the spring?"

"If it's a money issue, you don't have to worry. I'll cover your expenses."

"It's not a money issue." Her voice hardened. She backed away from him, walking to the windows over downtown Dunn. "That's six months of my life I didn't plan on surrendering."

"Dating awhile longer makes our engagement more believable," he countered. Everything in his life was falling into place. Losing Meghan too soon would be like removing the bottom card from that house of cards he'd so carefully crafted. "LA will be good for your career, too. I can introduce you to lots of new celebrities for your podcast. I meet them all the time."

Her eyes darted to him and then away. "I've been looking at houses in Dunn. I took on a sizable sponsor a few weeks ago, and requests for ad space have trickled in since. My podcast is gaining in popularity."

"You're welcome for that."

She glared.

"I'm not being an ass, Meghan. I'm trying to show you that this is what it means to be affiliated with me. More attention for the career you're building. For both of us. This has always been about us in this together. If you stay here, how's that us in this together?"

"My sister lives in Dunn. I just got her back."

He understood staying close to the ones you love, but… "It's only six months." He refused to take no for an answer. This was the next logical step. "You're a free agent, your podcast can be recorded from anywhere. I promise to fly Kendall and Max out to visit us."

"I like it here. I finally have my sister back, and my parents are close by. What makes you think I want to reacclimate to a strange city and work in a totally new environment while you're wherever you are doing whatever you're doing?"

He scratched his head, having no answer for that. He'd assumed she'd agree with him and say yes, and then they could handle wherever he'd be filming next as it came. She'd struck him as the nomadic type, since she rented a house and was suddenly available to stay in Dunn for the time being. Had he been wrong?

"I don't want to fight." He stroked her arms with his palms. "Take some time to think about it, okay? You'd like Los Angeles. We can attend the show's red-carpet premiere together. Imagine the publicity for your podcast. You'll be set for life. Then you can buy a giant house in Dunn, or anywhere in the world."

"You're not listening to me. I don't need to think about it," she clipped.

"Do it for me."

"Everything I've done lately has been *for you*. I wasn't exactly on board for this faux engagement, you know."

She was being the very definition of stubborn. Frustrated, he huffed, "You had no problem putting the ring on, moving in with me and sharing my bed."

"Unbelievable." She turned on her heel and stomped into the bedroom.

The door shut with a *snick*, leaving him standing by the windows, hands on his hips. That fight certainly hadn't felt fake. So, what did she expect? Two more weeks of living with him, of pretending to be engaged, and then they'd live on opposite coasts?

He'd have to attend the show's premiere by himself. The optics on that wouldn't be good. Everything had gone smoothly until now. What had changed?

As hard as he'd worked to reach this point in his career, he'd be damned if he'd watch it fall apart now. Granted, the success of the show didn't *hinge* on his being engaged to Meghan Squire, but their relationship was too important to let go so soon.

Everything had fallen apart once in his life, to disastrous consequences. Max leaving to pursue his own dreams had caused a domino effect that had left Isaac grappling for some semblance of normal for years. He wouldn't go through that again. He couldn't.

Not only for the sake of his career, but for his sanity. He deserved good things. And what about Meghan? Staying here might hold her back. She had momentum, and with the right connections they could build her an empire. Hell, a friend of his back home had recently sold his podcast for sixty million dollars. Sixty mil would be a windfall. She'd never have to work again.

She was smart, but inexperienced. Just because she didn't see the massive potential of returning to LA with him didn't mean he couldn't. She needed him, whether she liked it or not.

He'd find a way to prove it to her.

Thirteen

Three days. It'd been *three days* since he'd had sex with Meghan. It was beginning to appear as if the proverbial honeymoon was over, and they weren't even married.

Worse, they weren't snapping at each other, or openly arguing about whether or not she was moving to LA. Her mornings were rushed, with her gathering her laptop and planner and kissing him goodbye on her way to work at the coffee shop. By evening, she'd been parked in front of her laptop, headphones on, editing her latest podcast.

He'd planned on asking her about their abnormal dry spell until this morning, when he'd opened the bathroom cabinet and spotted a box of tampons on the shelf. That's when he realized she was on her period, which explained the lack of sex. She was still sore at him, but at least she wasn't repulsed by him.

God, he was an idiot.

He finished filming by one o'clock in the afternoon. Ashley told everyone to take the day and the next off since she'd like "some alone time with my sexy husband," who had come to town to visit. Isaac would take it. He could use the time to patch things up with Meghan, and hopefully sell her on the idea of California, after all.

"My last day." Outside of the hotel, Max expertly steered away from a group of fans with pens at the ready.

"You should sign something for them," Isaac urged, smiling and waving at the raised cell phones.

"Pass," Max said. "Let's get a beer. Then you can tell me what's been eating at you."

"What are you talking about?"

"It's me, Isaac. You know I know."

He probably did. They had always had that twin-mindmeld thing, and being close in proximity had amped it up tenfold. "Okay, but we have to go to your place or mine. I can't talk freely at Rocky's."

"My place," Max decided, angling for his truck.

Twenty minutes later, they arranged two Adirondack chairs around the bonfire Max had built in his backyard. Facing the mountainside, the crisp fall air cooling his lungs, Isaac was glad they hadn't gone to a restaurant to talk. The solitude of Max's place was nice. As if choreographed, they each lifted their beer bottles and sucked down hearty swallows.

"Damn, that tastes good." Max lowered into his chair.

"Tastes better because it's your last day of shooting." But his brother's last day wasn't entirely welcome to Isaac. That "whole feeling" was splintering yet again. With his and Meghan's distance, with Max wrapping his final scenes.

He hated this feeling. Brooding, he sat in his own chair and stared at the fire.

"Assuming your mood has something to do with Meghan," Max said.

"What mood?"

Max pointed at him. "That one."

Isaac gave in and explained his last argument with Meghan, concluding, "LA would be good for her."

"And for you."

"Well, yeah. But this has always been about helping each other. What's wrong with that?"

"Meghan doesn't want to live in LA any more than I do. Did she tell you she looked at a house out here?"

"She mentioned it." It irked him that Max knew, but then Max knew everything Kendall did so maybe Isaac shouldn't take it personally. "If she rents now, she'll settle for a tiny apartment. She can buy a giant house if she waits until the show airs. In six months she'll have ten times the fan base, which means bigger asks for sponsorships and bigger advertisers."

"Not everyone cares about *bigger*."

"It's smarter to continue the engagement story until the show airs."

"You're my brother and I love you," Max said, which harkened that a big-brother life lesson was forthcoming. "But if you break Meghan's heart, I'll crush you into tiny pieces."

"Meghan's heart is in zero danger. And you'd have your hands full with me, bro. I know tae kwon do."

Max's eyebrows jumped. "Really?"

"*Really*. Besides, Meghan is the one who wants to escape me, not the other way around."

"She's smart."

"Think you can give me your honest opinion without the insults?"

Contemplatively, Max took a swig from his beer bottle. Then he spoke.

"After they wrapped *Brooks Knows Best* the first time around, I made it clear to you that I wasn't interested in the spotlight any longer. You could not be deterred, brother. I wouldn't say you were blind with ambition, but you sure as fuck weren't seeing twenty-twenty. You dragged me to God knows how many signings and fairs so you could continue basking in the fading spotlight of your fans."

"I was passionate. You can't blame me for fighting as hard for it as you fought to escape it. And they were *our fans*." A point Max often forgot. "They loved you as much if not more than they loved me."

"Not true. You're the natural."

Not wanting to start an old argument that'd never ended well, Isaac sighed. "What does this have to do with Meghan?"

"She might be like me."

"Poorly shaven and grouchy at all hours of the day? Sorry to inform you, but she's not."

Max didn't so much as crack a smile. "She might define success differently than you do. Ambition is on a sliding scale. Not everyone wants ten times more in life."

Isaac started to argue how ridiculous that sounded, because who wouldn't want to be famous and crazy wealthy? Then he shut his mouth as he realized he was looking into the eyes of one man who didn't.

"I can't stay in Dunn," Isaac said. "What's on the line is too important to me." And leaving Meghan behind meant leaving behind an interlocking piece to his current life's puzzle. He needed them to stay together. At least for a while longer.

"So don't. Go back to LA after the show wraps. Do the auditions we both know Kendall will line up for you. In the meantime, Meghan will do her thing. Hollywood relationships rarely work out. Bloggers far and wide will report on the inevitable ending, and your fans will eventually forget you two ever dated."

A spike of regret lanced Isaac's chest. Ending his relationship with Meghan sounded even more bleak when Max said it.

"It's too soon," Isaac argued.

"It's not your place to tell her to leave Dunn, especially now that she and Kendall have reunited. Have you talked to her about her brother?"

Isaac nodded. She'd mentioned Quinton again since the first time he'd asked. The wound was a big one. Meghan had told him how hard it was growing up without Quinton, and how closed off Kendall had been for the years following his death. When Kendall went to

LA, Meghan had felt incomplete. A lot like Isaac had felt without Max.

"Kendall and Meghan have grown closer since Kendall's moved here," Max continued making his very valid point. "You might have a plan for your life, but you have to let Meghan do what's best for her, even if it means you're compromising."

Isaac wondered if his brother was talking about himself, as well. Max had walked away and had done what was best for him.

"You agreed to temporary with Meghan. What's it matter when it ends?"

"It just...does," Isaac answered lamely. She had become an integral part of this chapter of his life. He was making a comeback and she fit. When he'd lied about the girlfriend he didn't have on that talk show, he didn't expect to find a woman to slot into his life as seamlessly as Meghan. He liked coming home to her and seeing her on set. She had been supporting his dreams and goals from the beginning. Now it was all ending. The show, the relationship with Meghan. Isaac was returning to LA soon, and leaving his brother in Dunn. Everything was being ripped away.

Again.

Isaac watched the fire for a while, considering. He wasn't happy about the idea of leaving Meghan behind. He liked being with her. She made him better, more focused. He had a built-in support system. He could count on her sunny smiles and good-natured ribbing to brighten his day. At least that'd been the case before they'd had that stupid argument about LA.

He'd made the decision to convince her to come with him no matter the cost, but not speaking to the woman who turned him on both physically and mentally was too high a price to pay.

So, what the hell was he supposed to do? Giving up wasn't an option. But neither was continuing to argue with the one person who had his back.

"You okay?" Max asked.

"Yeah." Isaac nodded, knowing what he had to do. Rather than continuing to discuss his feelings, he opted to lighten the mood. "Just thinking about how full of shit you are."

"Oh, yeah?" Max, picking up on Isaac's easy tone, raised one eyebrow in challenge.

"No matter how you frame it in your head, you're famous, too. You're living in a town *your fans* named after you."

Max smiled easily. "Fine. You got me. You and I are both blind with ambition. Happy?"

Not yet. But Isaac would be. Just as soon as he apologized to Meghan for behaving like a horse's ass.

Kendall, after Meghan had pointed out how little time they'd been spending together, booked a spa day for them. Massages done, they were folded into fluffy white robes, green mud masks drying on their faces, their feet soaking in individual bubbly tubs meant to detoxify the bad juju in their bodies.

Meghan was full of bad juju, she wagered, given she and Isaac had been living together like ambivalent roommates for the past few days. Rather than actively argue with him, she'd been making excuses to leave the house or be busy with work whenever he was home. She slept next to him in bed, feigning fatigue and lying awake for hours before eventually falling asleep.

She hated it.

"Isaac wants me to move to LA," Meghan told her sister, unable to hold her tongue any longer. She'd hoped relaxing would help her forget why she'd been so upset, but he'd been the only thing on her mind during her shiatsu massage. "He wants us to—" Noting three other women in the room in various stages of pampering, Meghan censored herself. "He wants us to *be engaged* in LA."

"For real engaged?" Kendall whispered, and then her eyes widened as she caught Meghan's actual meaning. "Oh, *oh*. Got it." With an exaggerated wink, she continued. "Might as well live together until the wedding."

"Tone it down a little," Meghan whispered back. "I'm not going to LA."

"Why not?" her insane sister asked.

"Are you kidding? Wasn't it you who told me to 'be careful'?"

"Are you enjoying yourself?"

"Of course. Just…not in the same way you and Max enjoy yourselves."

Kendall's smile softened. "You could be."

Meghan automatically shook her head. "That's not what I want. I want to move to Dunn. Near you. My podcast is more profitable than ever before. Thanks, by the way." It was hard to admit when her sister was right, but Kendall had kicked open a door that could have taken months or years for Meghan to crack open by herself.

"I'd miss you, but you could find a lot more celebrities to interview in California. You could skyrocket your podcast into something monumental." Kendall's eyes sparkled with excitement. Her sister saw potential everywhere. That belief made Kendall a great talent agent.

"Is success all that matters to you?"

"No, of course not. But the move would be temporary, and you'd have fun there. I know it."

Meghan's stomach twisted. It would be fun until it wasn't. She didn't have the greatest track record with being responsible. She could handle her podcast growing a bit at a time. *Skyrocketing* sounded like more responsibility than she wanted to take on. Meghan was the fun, lighthearted, go-with-the-flow sister. She knew her limits.

"Isaac would be a great support system," Kendall said, seeming to echo Meghan's worry that she couldn't do it on her own. But she wanted to. She *needed* to.

What if she took on too many sponsors or advertisers? Would she feel boxed in, or like she couldn't create the kind of content she wanted? What if she grew too fast? What if the quality of the show suffered, and sponsors pulled out? It wasn't as if she could rely on Isaac Dunn to bail her out then. Theirs was a temporary arrangement, not a true partnership.

Rather than share her anxiety about Isaac or her podcast, she placed her hand on her sister's. "I just got you back. I don't want to relocate when you and I are finally close. That's why I was looking at the house in Dunn. You're happy for the first time since Quinton died. I don't want to miss a second of it."

"I have missed you, too. I love having you here. I just don't want to hold you back or make you live the life I'm living. You deserve to pursue your dreams." Kendall's eyes misted and overflowed, leaving streaks in her mud mask. She swiped her cheeks, leaving green residue on her fingers. "Oops."

"I am pursuing my dreams." Isaac was a part of that, but her sister was a bigger part. Meghan blinked away tears of her own. "I love you. You can trust that I know what I'm doing."

"I love you, too. And I do trust you. You are a grown woman capable of making her own decisions. I shouldn't try and persuade you into doing what I think is best. You totally have this."

Meghan's chest puffed up at her sister's vote of confidence. She was capable of succeeding her way. And that's exactly what she intended to do.

Isaac, script on his lap, sat on the balcony outside of the bedroom and watched the world go by. A few bystanders below had noticed him in passing. No one had attempted to photograph him, either thanks to the grainy darkness or because they didn't recognize his silhouette, he wasn't sure which.

He'd been reading his lines until it was too dark to make out the words. He'd since swapped that pastime for another: mulling over his life. Done contemplating, he stepped inside and locked the patio door behind him.

After talking to his brother, Isaac realized he'd been trying to control every nuance of his relationship with Meghan out of fear. Fear of losing the momentum he had in his career. Fear of losing everything again. It was so obvious now.

Meghan and Kendall had been at the spa all day, which had given him plenty of time to think about what to say when she returned home.

Home. Their temporary home. Everything about them was temporary and had been from the start. There was a part of him unwilling to accept that, but what choice did he have?

The front door opened, and in walked a fresh-faced, bright-eyed Meghan. Her smile was cautious instead of sunny, but it was there. "Hi."

"You're radiant. Did you have fun?" He approached her, unable to keep his distance. She was glowing, and he selfishly wanted some of her warmth for himself.

"I didn't know how stressed I was until the masseuse worked out a knot the size of a grapefruit." She rubbed her shoulder with one hand. "I might need an ice pack later."

"I haven't been helping with your stress level," he admitted. "I was wrong to try and force you to come to LA. I've been so focused on my career I forgot I wasn't the only one involved."

Relief swept through the room like a gentle breeze, and he noticed Meghan's shoulders relax. His next breath was easier to take, even after the concession he hadn't wanted to make. He couldn't force her to come with him to LA any more than he could have forced his brother to stay on the publicity train forever.

"You have a right to pursue your dreams your way. You don't owe me anything," he said.

"It's not that I don't want to be with you." She rested her hand on his chest, the barest of touches setting him ablaze. "I hope you know that being with you and getting to know you have meant so much to me."

"It's not over yet, Squire." This was starting to sound too much like goodbye for his taste. "We have wasted precious time lately arguing about this. My fault."

"I was being stubborn." She toyed with a button on his shirt. "Think we can make up for it? That lost time?"

"We can sure as hell try." He cupped the back of her head as she came a step closer. Inclining her chin, she met his gaze.

"Every inch of my skin has been salt-scrubbed and covered in oil." She licked her bottom lip, mischief creeping into her expression. "You won't believe how soft I am until you touch every inch of me."

"That sounds like an invitation." His voice was a low croak, tension tightening his vocal chords. He'd missed being with her like this. That naked vulnerability they shared in the solace of this apartment. He slipped his palms over her bare forearms. "You're right. Soft."

Her lips closed over his and his eyes shut of their own volition. She said his name, followed by, "I don't want to fight anymore."

"We won't." He reached for her shirt, and she lifted her arms. Everything was under control. She didn't have to come with him to LA. He'd finish filming here, continue making love to Meghan until he had to leave Virginia and then... Well, he wasn't sure what would happen next, but he knew what was happening right now.

"I've got you, Squire," he promised as he peeled away the rest of her clothes and his hands slipped along her oil-slicked skin.

He had her in his arms in this moment. And like she'd told him before, this moment was what counted.

Fourteen

Meghan had been granted an unexpected reprieve, which had arrived with the introduction of rewrites. The script upheaval had caused a delay, and had required additional shooting days, meaning Isaac would be staying longer than originally anticipated.

Over the next two weeks, she kept busy recording and editing podcasts with various members of the crew and cast. She'd popped in to the set several times, and it never failed to amuse her how accepted she'd become. She was Isaac's fiancée, and everyone loved him, so everyone she'd met so far automatically loved her.

She was beginning to feel as if she had an entire set of extended friends and family thanks to him. That this fantastical life was temporary was a hard pill to swallow. It was becoming difficult to look her newfound friends in the eyes and lie about her and Isaac's imaginary pending nuptials.

Tonight, he'd come home with his arms filled with takeout from an African-Asian fusion restaurant. Naan and several sauces for dipping, curried vegetables in coconut milk, rice and tandoori chicken infused the apartment with fragrant spices. The containers sat open on the coffee table. Meghan had filled her plate with a bit of everything.

He fired up the television, scrolling to a popular streaming app. "I have a surprise for you."

"If it's anything like the last surprise, I can't wait." A few days ago, he'd joined her in the shower and had lathered her up with body wash he'd received in a gift basket. He'd insisted on her honest opinion and, after a rubdown that had brought her to orgasm no fewer than twice, she'd given two very enthusiastic thumbs-up.

"I don't think any surprise could be that good." He grinned, catching her meaning. "Because of the *latest* script revisions, I have to rewatch a few classic Danny Brooks episodes."

"More changes?" She hated to hear that. He'd been cramming new lines into his head every evening and morning. He had to be tired of relearning scenes every other day.

"'Fraid so." He thumbed to season ten and chose an episode in the middle. "They're stepping up Danny's relationship with Rachael."

His on-screen girlfriend. She knew about Rachael's return—though she'd yet to meet the actress who played her. It felt strange to meet the woman Isaac spent time kissing on set. Come to think of it, that might be the real reason Meghan had avoided visiting the set lately.

"I know you've seen every episode three or four times, but I haven't." He pressed the play button. "In order to do justice to our scene tomorrow, I need the refresher."

"I haven't seen *every* episode multiple times," she defended. In fact, she'd skipped some of the episodes Rachael had been in. Particularly the kissing ones. Even before Meghan had known Isaac, she'd found watching him pretend to be in love with someone else unpleasant. She wrinkled her nose when the beautiful brunette's face filled the screen. Rachael was crying, and she looked incredible doing it.

"The most controversial episode ever." He canted an eyebrow. "The pregnancy scare."

That, she did recall. In the show's final season, they introduced a pregnancy scare. Danny and Rachael had lost their virginity to each other. The two-part episode let the outcome drag out and had managed to be dramatic without being preachy. Nevertheless, the episodes had caused a ruckus among more conservative viewers.

"I never understood the controversy." Isaac, his eyes on the screen, sounded contemplative. "It wasn't like we *actually* had sex."

"Thank goodness for that," Meghan grumbled as she tore a piece of naan and dunked it into yogurt sauce.

He paused the show, the screen frozen on his own handsome face. Even as a kid, Isaac Dunn had been dreamy. Thanks to the close-up, she could *just* make out the slim scar on his chin. No mistaking him for Max—that was Isaac, all right.

"What do you mean 'thank goodness'?" His smile reappeared as she scooped up a bite of rice and vegetables.

"It'd be awkward to be on set doing intimate things with Rachael if you actually *had* slept together."

"Sarabeth, you mean," he corrected, using the name of the actress with a familiarity Meghan didn't love. "If I'd actually slept with Sarabeth."

"Stop looking so amused by me."

"I can't help it." His smile broadened after he swallowed a bite of chicken. "You're cute when you're jealous."

"I'm *not* jealous," she lied. Badly. She preoccupied herself with her food. "I'm merely pointing out that you making out with Sarabeth on-screen would have been weird if you two had hooked up in real life."

"Making out?" He chuckled. "I'd hardly call what Sarabeth and I do on the show *making out*."

"It always looked intimate to me," Meghan mumbled around her next bite.

"It's supposed to look intimate. That doesn't mean it is."

"The other day I popped in to say hi, and you had one of *those scenes* with Rachael, and the whistles and woo-hooing were deafening."

"With Sarabeth."

"Sarabeth! Whatever."

"I'll be damned." He set down his fork. "I've never seen you like this, and I have to say, it's doing it for me."

She sputtered something about what an egomaniac he was and then added, "I'm not trying to *compliment* you."

"Am I to believe this reaction—" he gestured at her "—is out of professional interest?"

"Yes. You are to believe that."

"Well, I don't."

"Well, I'm sorry to hear that." She jutted her chin, daring him to argue. He did her one better. Bracketing her body with both fists, he leaned over her and maneuvered his hips between her legs.

"Why don't I explain what kissing Sarabeth-slash-Rachael is like on set. Purely for research purposes, of course."

"No thanks." The last thing she wanted to hear was what it was like for him to kiss another woman. He might be hers for only a little while, but he was hers until he wasn't. She didn't want to share him in the meantime.

The smirk resting on his perfect mouth didn't go anywhere. "TV kisses aren't like real kisses, Squire. You can't trust the audience's reaction. They love romance. You should have heard the whistles when Richard and Merilyn kissed the other day."

"You don't have to lie to make me feel better."

"I swear I'm not. Come on, let me show you." He nudged her nose with his. This close to him, she wouldn't say no. He touched his mouth to hers, opening her lips. When she expected his tongue to stroke hers and make her forget the world around her, he ended the kiss with a soft smooch.

Before she could ask what that was about, he dove

in again, this time more aggressively. His mouth was open, so was hers, but whenever she tried to touch her tongue with his, he backed off. The fire she was used to feeling between them was there, but somehow... *different*. He kissed her bottom lip and then the top, finishing her off with another invasion of her mouth that was anything but.

"Well?" he rumbled, his lips an inch away from hers.

She gave him an unsure half smile. "What the hell was that?"

"An as-seen-on-TV kiss. Are you overcome with passion?"

"Not really," she admitted.

"Imagine a packed set. An audience whistling, three cameras pointed directly at you. You're thinking about how to stay on your mark, where to hold your head so you don't block your costar's close-up." He dipped his voice into a low sensual husk. "Am I turning you on yet?"

She was starting to see his point. "No, I guess not."

"No. You guess not." The heat returned to his eyes. "When I kiss you, though..."

He leaned in for another kiss, but this time he didn't hold back. She got tongue, and a lot of it. Even the way he cupped her jaw and stroked his fingers into her hair was intimate. This kiss was raw, real. It was just for them and their enjoyment and there was nothing po-lite about it.

He slipped his tongue against hers, pressing her body deep into the couch cushions. By the time he tried to finish the kiss with a tug of his teeth to her bottom lip, she was clinging to him, her arms and legs wrapped around every available part of him.

"I've never kissed Sarabeth that way." He kept his focus on her face while he ran his knuckles over her breast and up again, teasing her nipple beneath her thin cotton shirt. "And this sort of touching is way too hot for our show."

Clutching his neck, she tugged his mouth to hers and tilted her hips. Brazen from his earlier exploration, she didn't hold back when she challenged, "Show me what other moves you *haven't* done with Sarabeth."

"You sure?" he asked cockily. "There are a lot of them. We can't possibly do them all in one night."

"Maybe not." She bit his lip, then soothed it with a gentle lick. "But we can try."

Fifteen

A flash of lightning lit the bedroom and woke Meghan out of a deep sleep. Thunder rattled the windowpanes a second later as fat raindrops slapped the glass. Her eyes flew open, her brain clinging to the vestiges of a dream she couldn't remember.

She lay there for a moment, her heart racing. Rain rolling down the windows was shadowed on the ceiling overhead. Anxiety coated her, bringing with it the uncomfortable sensation that she'd missed something important.

She shook her head, dismissing what must've been a nightmare. She rerouted her attention to more pleasant thoughts, like what had happened a few hours ago. Isaac had made love to her on the couch, their dinners forgotten. His hands had been everywhere at once and she'd let him do what he pleased, her eyes rolled back in ecstasy the entire time. He'd held and kissed her for a long while after they'd had sex. And then they'd sat up, reclaimed their forks and chatted while finishing off their dinner.

He was incredible. Incredibly hot and funny and… temporary.

Her smile faded. Maybe that was the source of her anxiety. Even though they'd planned for their time together to end, the closer the end came, the less ready she was to call it quits. She would miss him when he was gone. And not just the great sex, though she'd have to channel her sexual energy into something productive. She'd miss talking to him, too. Listening as he excitedly told her about his day. Helping him practice his lines. Sharing dinners and coffees or rare midday naps.

She'd miss *him*. All of him.

Remarkably, Isaac slept through the storm, his back to her, his shoulder exposed, his chest rising and falling in a steady rhythm. Would he miss her as much as she'd miss him? Would he miss her at all?

Giving up on falling asleep any time soon, she tossed off her blankets and padded into the attached bathroom. She splashed her face with cool water and was patting her cheeks dry with a hand towel when the sense of dread returned.

She thought back to the show they'd watched where Rachael had agonized over an unexpected pregnancy. Isaac had paused the episode often to discuss how he planned to honor the past between their characters in order to make sure the present-day material was authentic. Meghan had been less jealous than before, given the care he'd taken to set her mind at ease. She'd mostly been fascinated by his process and by how much was involved in rekindling a love interest on the show.

She wasn't thinking of that now, though. She was thinking of unexpected pregnancies on a more personal level. She yanked open the cabinet beneath Isaac's sink to find an unopened box of tampons staring up at her. Her heart thrashed as reality descended, thorny and mocking.

She hadn't used a single one.

She hadn't needed to yet.

She shut the cabinet doors with shaking hands. She'd been busy. She'd been stressed. She was as far from her normal routine as possible. A late period had happened to her before, and it hadn't amounted to anything.

She tiptoed back into the bedroom to grab her cell phone from the nightstand. Once she was seated on the couch, memories of making love to Isaac returned. He'd used a condom tonight—he'd used a condom every time they'd been together save that first time. What were the odds?

Meghan wished she were the type of woman organized enough to track her period on her phone's calendar, but *alas*. She searched online for "reasons for a missed period" and, other than pregnancy, there were actually a lot of them. Stress and routine upset were at the top.

Maybe it was nothing?

Chewing on her fingernail, she debated what to do next. Panicking wasn't helping. Worrying wouldn't bring a solution. There was nothing she could do until morning anyway. She watched out the window as the rain fell, trying desperately to blank her mind. Eventually, she must have, because her eyes grew heavy and she fell asleep.

Hours later, she woke to a kiss on her cheek. Isaac was standing over her, dressed in gray sweats and nothing else. Sunshine streamed into the living room. The storm had subsided. Disoriented, she rubbed her eyes.

"You slept in here at some point, I see. Was I snoring?"

"No. The storm woke me up. Besides, I can sleep through snoring. Kendall and I used to share a bedroom."

"Kendall snores?" Isaac tossed his head back and laughed. "Oh, man. I'm using that against her. You can't stop me."

She managed a pained smile as he padded to the kitchen. That same feeling of dread that woke her in the night coated her anew. She wouldn't rest until she knew for sure if she was pregnant.

God. Pregnant.

"Coffee?" Isaac offered, holding up an empty mug.

"Uh, no thanks. Water would be better." Especially if the unthinkable had happened.

"Out of the usual for you, but I'll allow it." He delivered a glass of cold water, teased her about how she should have woken him up if she was afraid of "a little rain" and sat down to turn on the show they'd stopped in the middle of last night. *Brooks Knows Best*, season ten, episode nine.

That quaking feeling returned to her belly as Rachael mentioned the "close call" with what could have been a baby for her and Danny.

Close call.

Had Meghan and Isaac had a similar close call? And if so, what the hell would she do about it? Obviously, she loved him, but a baby was next level. Plus—

Water glass halfway to her lips, she froze.

She loved him.

Because of course she did.

He had been her favorite actor when she was young, and he was one of her favorite people now. Isaac Dunn was a spectacularly nice guy with talent to spare. Roll in his epic kissing skills and the way he treated her in bed and out of it, and there was nothing not to love about him.

"I have to go soon. You good here?" He stood from the couch.

She nodded, but she wasn't staying here. The second he left his apartment, she was going to leave, too. But rather than follow him to set, she was going straight to the drugstore to buy a pregnancy test.

Maybe two.

Isaac noticed that Sarabeth had been in a bright, sunshiny mood the moment she'd arrived on set. She brought with her the nostalgia of the days past, when they'd rehearsed and filmed together. Now, in the middle of shooting a dramatic scene, that Sarabeth was long gone. She'd been replaced by a drawn and muted Rachael. Sadness ebbed off her and adhered to him, making it easier to genuinely react to her character's mood.

She was a damn good actress.

She'd aged beautifully, losing the pregnancy weight from her second and third children—twins. And, Isaac knew because they'd discussed it at the table read, it'd taken a few rounds of hormones for her to be able to *get* pregnant that second time. She'd told him she was planning on using her heartbreak from years of being unable to conceive and pouring it into the tough scene they were performing right this very moment.

"Just like old times," she said, her smile wistful. "Except this time, I wished with all my heart to be pregnant."

"I know." He held her upper arms, giving her as much emotion as he was able so that she could use it for her performance. As if the audience had sensed her vulnerability, a hush had fallen over the set.

"Are you relieved?" Hope filtered into her expression.

"No." He took a breath. "But we'll have plenty of other opportunities to try. I'm not letting you leave, Rachael. Never again."

"I can't be sure of that."

"You can." From his pocket, he extracted a ring. The props department had scrambled to find a replacement for the missing ring. He'd stayed resolutely silent about its whereabouts.

As Danny, he proposed to his on-screen partner. His character had lost the woman he loved and had been granted a rare second chance. "Rachael, I love you. I've loved you for half my life. If you marry me, I promise to love you for the other half—for the rest of it. We'll do whatever it takes to have a baby together. We'll do whatever it takes to be *a family*."

"Oh, Danny." Sarabeth's eyes misted over as she delivered one of her patented pretty cries. She hugged him, and he shifted slightly to ensure that she was in frame of the camera over his left shoulder. Then she said the line he knew would win over any audience. "We're already a family."

She pulled away, his cue to go in for the kind of TV kiss he'd demonstrated for Meghan last night. He slipped the ring onto her finger and then pressed his lips to his costar's. As predicted, the audience went wild.

Ashley yelled cut. Sarabeth snapped out of the scene, dried her eyes and broke into a huge grin. The applause was deafening as they clasped hands and took a bow. They'd nailed it.

As he scanned the packed crowd, he was surprised to spot Meghan in the front row. She hadn't told him she'd planned on watching today's filming. What a nice surprise.

He kept hold of Sarabeth's hand and towed her over to Meghan, saying, "There's someone I want you to meet."

His fiancée stood when they approached. She was fresh and beautiful in a cream-colored sweater, jeans and boots. She twisted her fingers like she was nervous. Isaac felt for her, he did. Even though she knew the kiss between him and his costar had been for show, he sure as hell wouldn't like to see Meghan kiss another man.

"Meghan Squire, this is Sarabeth Commons. You might know her better as Rachael."

"It's so wonderful to meet you." Sarabeth extended a hand. Meghan hesitated, her expression strained. An ice pick of worry lodged itself in his chest until Meghan slapped on a smile and shook the other woman's hand.

"You, too."

"Meghan was a huge fan of the show back when we were acting our prepubescent hearts out," he told Sarabeth.

"I'm so embarrassed about my hairstyle and clothes back then." Sarabeth smiled. "I heard you have a podcast about the show. That is so exciting."

"She's been lining up interviews with everyone on set. She's an amazing interviewer. Generous, funny," he bragged. To Meghan, he said, "Sarabeth already told me she'd do it. She has toddler twins at home, but vowed to make the time."

"Heck, I'll do it *because* I have toddler twins at home!" Sarabeth laughed. "Eric is great with them. And my daughter is finally at an age where she can help. And by 'help' I mean entertain herself."

Ashley stepped into their tight circle and crowed about how "incredible" Isaac and Sarabeth were in the scene they'd just shot. "Sarabeth, come watch the playback with me."

"Sure thing. Meghan, we'll get together soon."

Meghan offered a nod as the other two ladies walked across the soundstage.

"Everything all right?" he asked once they were gone. Something was off. His Spidey senses were tingling.

"When are you done?" she asked.

"That was it for me. I don't have any other scenes to film today. Do you want to grab a bite to eat?"

"Actually..." She twisted her fingers again, sending adrenaline coursing through his veins. "Can we take a walk?"

Sixteen

Meghan led the way into the hotel lobby as Isaac rushed to keep up with her long-legged steps. She was on a mission, to do what he had no idea.

Outside, he was stopped by a group of five women he'd come to think of as his personal fan club. Their timing was horrible, but they didn't know that.

"Ah, Meghan," he started, but she picked up on what to do before he reminded her. She pasted on a smile that didn't quite reach her eyes and stepped slightly behind him to give him room to talk.

He signed five matching bright pink T-shirts, with his screen-printed face and the words *We're not Dunn yet!* encircling the photo. Then he stayed long enough for the women to snap selfies before excusing himself. Thankfully, no one followed as he and Meghan strode up the hill.

"How's the park?" She sent a furtive look around, he guessed, checking for more of his fans.

"Yeah, that's fine. Looks empty. You sure you're okay?"

"Not really."

His heart was lodged in his esophagus, his hand sweating in hers. Was she upset about him kissing Sarabeth? Had she decided to leave Dunn sooner than they'd discussed? Had something awful happened to one of their siblings?

That thought sent his stomach to his feet like an elevator car with the cables cut.

"Hey." He stopped walking. "Is Max okay?"

Her eyebrows closed in over her cute nose. "Yes."

She led him to a bench at the edge of the park. Their shoes crunched the leaves strewn on the ground. By the time they sat down, he was filled with dread and not sure why.

"What about Kendall? Your parents?" he asked.

"Everyone is fine."

"Then what's going on?"

She bit her bottom lip before meeting his eyes. "Remember how your cousin had to try multiple times to get pregnant?"

His face went cold. "Yes."

"We didn't. Once, apparently, was enough."

Good thing he'd sat down. The strength had left his legs and probably wouldn't return for a while.

"Are you…?" He couldn't say it aloud. His brain was processing the news as slowly as possible.

"Pregnant," she said for him. "Yes."

For a few dramatic seconds, the whooshing of his heartbeat in his ears was the only sound he heard.

"You can't be," he said through numb lips. He'd planned his life out. He'd picked the perfect woman for a fake relationship, which had nothing to do with a baby on board, by the way. Desperately, he reminded her, "There is a box of feminine…thingies under my sink."

He prayed she'd jump in and say something like, *"Oh my gosh! I totally forgot! I'm not pregnant, after all."* Oh, how they'd laugh…

Instead, she stared at him.

"Did you take a…uh, did you buy a test?"

"Yes. I both bought and took a test."

"Maybe you should buy another one?"

"Should I buy three? Because that's how many I took."

"And they were positive."

"Yes, Isaac." Her impatience was evident, but he was trying here. Trying to wrap his head around the fact that she was pr-pruh… Damn. He couldn't even think it now. "I forgot the number one rule while having an affair. Looks like I'm going to live up to everyone's low expectations of me after all."

"I forgot, too, Squire," he reminded her. He put his palm to his forehead, his brain spinning. He wasn't sure what to address first. The fact that she worried about others thinking her irresponsible, or the fact she'd purchased *three* tests and learned she was pregnant… Ha! There. He was able to think the word after all.

His smile fell as another possibility entered the picture and gave him the finger.

Oh, shit.

"Where?" he asked.

"Where did I take the tests? In your bathroom." She frowned, misunderstanding him.

"No... Where did you *buy* the tests?" Had she ordered them online two days ago without telling him? Had she driven out of Dunn to a nearby town and worn a disguise? Or had she done the unthinkable, and purchased them here *in Dunn*, where any number of fans of the show could have witnessed her doing it?

"Oh. At the market."

"The market in Dunn." The numbness spread from his lips to his entire body.

"Yeah, so?"

"So?" He laughed, the sound half-crazed. He shot a glance over his shoulder and then hers to determine they were actually alone. "Who saw you buy the tests?"

"Uh..."

"*Think.* It's important."

"The important takeaway is that you and I are expecting, Isaac."

"You're wrong," he snapped, even as he argued with himself that this wasn't her fault. This was mostly his fault. He'd had everything under control until he'd had her naked and beneath him, which had led to an oversight that had changed everything.

"Why do you care who saw me?"

She wasn't in the public eye. She didn't know how ruthless the press could be. How social media could bury him before his publicist had a chance to control the spin.

"There are a lot of people in Dunn who are interested in the show and me. And you, Meghan. *Because* of who I am."

"Isaac—"

"Have you checked the internet to see if you were photographed?"

"Why would I do that?"

"Everything we've worked for up until this point could be on the line." He was fucked if he didn't get control of how this news spread.

She grabbed his face, her palms on each of his cheeks, and forced his gaze to hers. "Are you hearing yourself? Screw the press, the show and the fans. Isaac, I'm pregnant. With a baby. That's the headline here."

He opened his mouth to say "I know" when the word *baby* ricocheted around his head. Meghan Squire was pregnant with a baby. *His* baby.

Holy hell.

He pushed his fingers into his hair, his eyes unfocused on the mountains in the distance. Then she said something that snapped him out of it.

"My entire life is about to change."

"Not just yours." He took her hands in his. "We're in this together, Squire. Just like we have been from the beginning."

"Back when we were temporary."

That was true. They'd never been in this together permanently. From the beginning, it'd been an arrangement made with their careers coming first. When it'd turned physical, he'd convinced himself their shared attraction was a fun bonus. But now…everything had changed.

A baby.

He'd shot a scene today about not being able to conceive, and here Meghan sat, telling him she was pregnant. The truth really was stranger than fiction. His plans to move away and her plans not to come with him would need reevaluating.

He nodded, the unexpected news finally taking root. "There's nothing temporary about a baby."

"You assume I'm keeping the baby."

He pulled her into focus, his heart aching. He had assumed that. It was the only assumption. "Listen, I hadn't planned on becoming a father, and I'm sure you hadn't planned on becoming a mother. This soon, anyway." He cleared his throat, unsure how much to say but compelled to say it. "Meghan, I'm equipped to handle it. Even if I'm not exactly ready."

Her smile was soft, her voice soothing as she touched his cheek. "I know you are. I can't imagine not having this baby even though I'm shocked and unprepared."

He blew out a breath of relief as a million questions swirled around inside his head. What did this mean for their future? Their careers? Nothing was certain from here on out. Their temporary fling for fun had suddenly become more than either of them had intended.

"What about the photographs?"

"What photographs?" he asked.

Her eyebrows lifted. "The ones that could have been taken of me in the market when I was buying the tests."

Oh. Those. Funny how that'd been his first concern. He'd been in shock. In spin mode. He'd been trouble-shooting. He'd cared about nothing but his own career for too long. Everything he'd done lately had been in service to *Brooks Knows Best*. Well, no more. He had more to think about than a TV show. He was about to have a family of his own.

That didn't change the fact that the photos, if there were any, needed to be handled. They couldn't ignore the press once speculation began, or the blowback that would inevitably follow.

"Unfortunately, we do need to talk about what to do if those photos exist. And probably make a statement of some sort."

Meghan chewed her lip. Then she and Isaac concluded at the same time, "Kendall."

Seventeen

Rust orange, golden yellow and green rushed by the car window as Isaac drove up the wooded mountainside to his brother's house. Meghan had been silent during the short drive, watching the colorful landscape whisk by the window. He let her have a moment. Hell, he needed a few himself.

She was pregnant. She was keeping the baby. He was going to be a father. The facts had finally sunk in, but dust from the atom bomb hadn't completely settled yet.

She was going to be in his life forever. No takebacks. No temporary about it. Even if they never saw one another romantically again, he'd forever be the father of their child. She'd forever be their child's mother. After foolishly believing he was in control of his life, he was witnessing parts of it careening off the edge of a cliff. He kept his eyes on the road so that he didn't do the same with the car.

Max's house came into view, the setting sun bathing the luxury cabin in a warm orange hue. At first Isaac had thought his brother crazy for moving from LA to the sticks, but after he'd visited Dunn, he understood why Max chose to settle here.

There was something inviting and homey about this town. Nature surrounded them on all sides, below and above. The changing seasons, from rainbow-colored wildflowers to pure white snow on the mountaintops, were majestic to behold. Dunn was a great place to raise a family.

Isaac hadn't planned on raising a family anywhere, let alone in LA, but people did it all the time. At least, he assumed they did. He pictured moving to Dunn and cringed. As beautiful as this town was, he hadn't planned on retiring this soon, either. He and Meghan would have to find a solution together. But first things first. They had to tell Kendall what had happened.

He parked in the driveway and rounded the car to let Meghan out. By the time he was on her side of the vehicle, she was already halfway up the walk. He caught her hand before she stepped onto the porch. No matter what happened inside, he was here for her. He gently squeezed her fingers and, as if she understood, she nodded. They walked up the steps of the front porch together.

"Oh my God!" Meghan shrieked, dropping his hand to cover her mouth.

A glass door separated them from the scene inside.

A candlelit dinner. Flutes of champagne. Max on one knee, a ring held up in offering to Kendall.

"Oh my God," Isaac echoed.

Then the four of them just…stared at each other in shock.

Meghan recovered first, throwing open the door while repeating, "Ohmygod! Oh my God!"

Isaac caught the door before it could shut in his face. He stepped inside behind her, nodding at his brother as Max stood from his kneel to take in the melee around him.

Kendall embraced her sister, laughing. Meghan offered an apology for interrupting and expressed how happy she was for them.

Isaac read Max's expression clearly, and it was asking, *What the hell are you doing here?*

Long story.

Well, it better be good.

Don't worry, brother. It is.

"What are you two doing here?" Kendall asked aloud. Meghan sobered, nodding at Isaac as they both sat down at the table.

"Um…" Meghan looked to him for help. He could read her expression, too, and it appeared to be asking, *Line?*

"Since you're my agent," Isaac said to Kendall.

"You're here for a work matter?" Max boomed, a displeased line where his mouth used to be. There was beard and more beard. No lips to speak of.

"It's bigger than that," Isaac told him. Then to Kendall, "Gossip has a way of making it to you before me, and I don't want you to be caught unawares."

"Unawares of what?" Kendall's eyes flicked to her sister and then back to him. "What happened?"

"As you know, Isaac and I have been...dating," Meghan jumped in. "And living together."

Kendall's face scrunched. "Yeah. I know."

"Well...we've also been doing other things couples do when they are living together. Alone. With ample access to the entire house." Meghan nodded meaningfully.

"Yeah, I figured," Kendall said with a low laugh. Then her smile dropped slowly, realization dawning in her eyes. "Oh God. Did you— Are you—"

Meghan nodded. "I'm afraid so."

Kendall rested her hand on her forehead much like Isaac had done when he found out. Her engagement ring glinted in the candlelight, reminding him of what they'd interrupted.

"What the hell's going on?" Max looked from Kendall to Meghan to Isaac.

"Meghan's pregnant," Isaac said. "With my baby."

Max's attention was solely on Isaac now. His brow darkened, his shoulders stiffened. Isaac mentally prepared for his brother to attempt to make good on the promise he'd made to crush Isaac into tiny pieces.

Instead, Max looked to Kendall and said something none of them expected. "You didn't answer me."

Kendall pulled her hand from her head. "Sorry?"

Max took her left hand in his and showed her the ring. "I ended my speech—the one about how much I love you and how I deserve to have you in my life every day—with a conclusion. I told you I never saw myself getting married again. And then I gave you this." He thumbed the ring on her finger.

Kendall smiled. "You didn't ask me a question, Max."

"It was implied, California," he muttered.

"You still have to *ask*."

He took a breath, considered his unexpected company and then murmured to Kendall, "Will you marry me?"

Again, Meghan shrieked.

"Of course I will, silly," Kendall answered, kissing Max's bearded frown.

He stood and scooped Kendall into his arms, and then hauled her to the staircase. "Bye, kids!"

"Wait, wait." Kendall laughed as she tapped his shoulders. "They can't leave."

"Yes, they can."

"No." Kendall squirmed until Max gave up and set her on her feet. She straightened her sweater and then her hair before sending him a playful eye roll. "We have to strategize. After we strategize, they'll leave. And then you and I can spend the evening doing anything you want."

"Anything?" Max asked.

"Anything," Kendall promised.

Max let out a gusty sigh and then said to Isaac, "Make it fast."

Kendall was the organized Squire sister. The planner. The *strategizer*.

Meghan had managed to pull off living on her own, and somewhat building her career on her own, but she'd managed to overlook a tiny detail that had landed her in hotter water than ever before. *A baby.*

There was no hotter water than pregnancy.

She didn't have a lot of experience with babies—any, actually, unless she counted the one time she'd held her cousin's infant son about three years ago. Meghan knew that babies had a way of eclipsing your whole life. They needed constant care. Stability. A mother and a father.

Whenever she thought of the words *mother* and *father*, she called up images of her parents. Parents were older, more responsible people. Parents did not hearken an image of a podcaster and a former child star. How would she and Isaac manage to do any of this, separate but present, for their child?

"I've got it," Kendall blurted.

Meghan had never been so happy to hear her sister's confident tone. She'd been searching the internet on her laptop at the kitchen table for the last fifteen minutes, the half-eaten plates from her and Max's fancy steak dinner pushed to the side.

"What do you got?" Isaac asked from his position at the kitchen island. Max was standing next to him, knife vertical over a pan of homemade marble brownies.

"She can say they were for me." Kendall grinned at Meghan. "You can say you were buying the pregnancy tests for me. I'm the perfect alibi."

"And when she starts showing, then what?" Isaac asked. "Want us to say she's carrying your baby, too?"

"No, smart-ass. This will buy you time while you figure out what you're doing."

"It's more lying," Max said. "What did we agree on,

California? No more lying. You and Isaac tried that already and look where we've ended up."

Meghan felt her cheeks grow hot.

"Not talking about you, Meg," Max soothed when he noticed her embarrassment.

"It's a good idea." Kendall placed her hand on Meghan's. "You were photographed buying pregnancy tests, by the way."

She flipped around her laptop to show a photo of Meghan, wearing the same outfit she wore now, with a Clearblue Easy pregnancy test in hand. Kendall scrolled down to another photo at the checkout counter, and another of Meghan, shopping bag in hand, walking into the deli beneath Isaac's apartment.

"There is a lot of speculation." Kendall shut the laptop. "Everyone has concluded you're pregnant."

"They're not wrong," Meghan murmured.

"Are you ready to tell the public?" Kendall asked. "Are you ready to tell Mom and Dad?"

"What will *you* tell Mom and Dad?" Meghan shot back.

"I'll tell Mom and Dad what I'll tell everyone else. It was negative and the press blew it out of proportion like they do everything else. By the time you're showing, we'll be more prepared to announce it. If you're in the public eye by then."

Kendall's gaze went over Meghan's head to Isaac. When Meghan turned to look at him, his mouth pulled into a frown. No one asked the obvious question, but it had to be on everyone's mind. Were Isaac and Meghan going to go through with the breakup? Had the pregnancy changed anything? She was in love with him, but she hadn't told him. Why bother if he was halfway out the door?

God, what a mess.

"She's right," Meghan told Isaac. "No one will care who I am by then. Living in Dunn doesn't make any sense. I could be living closer to Mom and Dad, who will be super excited to help."

"I can help," Kendall argued. "You can still move to Dunn. I want you here."

"Ken—"

"She's right," Max added. "We can help with the baby. We want you here."

"It's my baby," Isaac interrupted. "I'll be the one *helping*."

"You'll be in LA," Meghan reminded him.

"She's not moving to LA now that she's pregnant," Kendall snapped.

"My life—my career—is in LA," Isaac said.

"And what about my career?" Meghan snapped.

"Your career could be there, too."

"We discussed this already." Meghan shut her eyes. "I'm not moving to the other side of the country, especially now."

"You don't have to decide today," Kendall said. "I'll fall on the grenade initially, which will give you two time to work out a plan. And that plan will involve Meghan living here. With us, if she needs to."

"Don't worry, Max," Meghan assured him when his mouth dropped open, presumably to argue. "I'm not moving in with you guys. I'm going to find my own place." To her sister, she continued, "I'm done lying. The timing is not ideal, but this baby is on its own timeline. If the world knows I'm pregnant with Isaac's child, then they just do. Mom and Dad are going to find out eventually."

Meghan planned on sharing the truth with them. About the fake engagement and the relationship with Isaac, which, to be fair, was real for a while. She'd leave out how she'd fallen in love with him. She wasn't ready to admit that to anyone. What was the point? He was leaving.

He'd made it clear that his career came first. She wouldn't stand in the way of his success. She could handle a child—she had to. "I can do this, Ken. I appreciate the offer, but I don't need you to cover for me. I know I haven't always been the most responsible person, and I know you think I make a mess of things…"

"Oh, honey, I don't think that," her sister interrupted. "I'm trying to help in my own loving, bossy way. You are going to be the best mom ever. And I am going to be the best aunt ever."

"You are," Meghan said with a smile. "Will you promise to color-code the nursery?"

Kendall drew an X over her chest. "Cross my heart."

"Okay, then. It's settled." Meghan stood from the table and pointed at the brownies Max was carving into perfect squares. "Can I have one of those to go?"

"Sure thing, Meg." He bagged up her dessert.

Isaac watched, saying nothing, his expression revealing as much.

Eighteen

The elusive wholeness Isaac sought had splintered again, but not with his career or his relationship with Max. No, this time, it was with Meghan. Meghan, who'd been temporary. Meghan, who'd refused to relocate to LA. Meghan…the mother of his child.

Isaac's plans to be a Hollywood go-to, to live a life of his wildest dreams, and finally land a movie role seemed shallow in comparison. A baby was a life-changer. The fun and sexy relationship with Meghan was meant to come to an end, but now…now what? She was more than the mother of his child. She was the woman he wanted.

For more than temporary.

The night they'd left Max and Kendall, Isaac and Meghan had shared a silent ride back to his place. Isaac had heard everything she'd said to his brother and future sister-in-law and agreed with none of it. Meghan living in Dunn, away from him, while his child grew in her belly, was a reality he couldn't wrap his head around. But after the blowup between them over her moving to LA the first time, he didn't dare bring it up again so soon.

Now, though, after a few careful days together where they'd retreated to neutral corners, it was time to talk about the baby elephant in the room.

Sarabeth, next to him at the table read, said Rachael's line and pulled him back to the current moment. "Besides, we were planning on moving next door."

Richard, on cue, grinned like a proud father.

"No, no," Isaac read, holding up a hand to express his horror. "We were thinking we'd move far, far away."

Ashley and one of the writers chuckled. He'd landed the joke, remarkably. He hadn't felt funny this morning when he'd left a contemplative, quiet Meghan in his apartment.

"Don't listen to him, Dad," Sarabeth as Rachael cooed.

"I like when you call me Dad," Richard said. "You can't take her away from us, Danny. She's just come back."

"And we have a lot of shopping for the wedding to do," Merilyn chirped, ever the overinvolved mother character.

"That sounds expensive," Isaac mumbled.

"It won't be so bad, honey." Sarabeth palmed his arm. "You only get married once."

"Unless you're her sister." Richard shot a thumb toward Merilyn. "What number's Amy on now, honey? Baker's dozen?"

Merilyn swatted Richard on the arm, as per the script's instruction. "Oh, stop it. We're going to leave you kids to do whatever it is you do when parents aren't here."

"Parents leave," Ashley read from the script. "Rachael and Danny embrace."

Everyone at the table turned the page on their scripts. His line was next.

"I'm not moving next door to my parents. They'll drive us crazy. Grab our mail out of the box and hand-deliver it. That's a federal offense, you know."

Laughter rippled around the table.

"Fine, I get it." Sarabeth rolled her eyes. "You need distance."

"From everyone but you," he read. "I know I've screwed up a lot, but from now on, no more screwups. I'm going to prove to you that you can count on me. I will give you everything you need. You'll never want for anything again."

"Passionate kiss," Ashley read. "Danny and Rachael exchange adoring gazes."

"There's only one thing left to do, I guess." Sarabeth sighed.

"Agreed," Isaac read. "Let's go to the bedroom."

"No, not that." She laughed. "I'm talking about you writing your vows. I want to hear all the ways you can't live without me."

"Oh, no. No, no. The ones the church provides will get us just as married as whatever drivel I come up with."

"You did say you would provide *anything* I needed."

"And you need vows?" He winced.

"Rachael falls quiet," Ashley read. "Danny realizes he owes her more than the promise of a fancy wedding. He owes her his heart."

"You need vows," Isaac said. "Okay, then." He reached over to hold Sarabeth's hand as the script suggested. "I saw a pen and paper in the nightstand drawer. How about we start there?"

"Always the joker." Sarabeth shook her head.

"I'm not… I'm not great at this stuff, Rachael. Saying what I mean. It's hard for me to express my feelings." His heart pounded as he considered what a true statement that was. For how long had he not been able to tell Meghan how he felt about their situation? "I love you. I'm ready to say that."

"That's a fantastic start. I love you, too."

"Does that count as vows?"

"Not on your life," Sarabeth read, deadpan. Everyone around the table laughed on cue.

"Worth a shot, I guess."

"And…scene," Ashley announced. "Well done, everyone. How did that feel?"

"I feel good about it," Sarabeth said. "It allows them to be serious and light at once. They've been through a lot together and you believe they're going to make it."

Isaac thought of him and Meghan. They were light and then serious, but he couldn't seem to reach the fun-loving, easygoing version of her lately. Was there a corner to turn? A solution that made a baby another exciting piece of their lives together? Or would it forever divide them, just as LA and Dunn had divided them?

"Isaac?" Ashley prompted.

He blinked at the director, aware he'd taken a mental vacation for a few seconds. "It's perfect. The script wraps up Danny and Rachael nicely but leaves room for a Christmas reunion show. Anyone?"

"Yes, please!" Sarabeth said. Richard and Merilyn voiced their agreement as well.

"Let's release this reboot first, and then we'll plan all the things," Ashley promised. "That's it for today, kids. See me if you have any questions about the script."

They made their way out of the conference room, everyone save Isaac marching to the food cart to grab lunch. He was planning on going home to talk to Meghan about their options. There had to be middle ground. Maybe he could stay in Dunn until he needed to audition elsewhere. He'd fly back and forth to stay with her. Not to convince the press, but because she was important to him. She was carrying his child. They were going to be a family.

There was no other option.

They got along well...when they weren't arguing over geography. And, they had time. That was the most important part. It wasn't like he'd have to fly to LA immediately.

He pulled his cell phone from his pocket, noticing a missed call from Kendall. No voice mail. His heart hit his feet as he excused himself from the room. Given his and Meghan's current tumultuous state, he wasn't sure Kendall was calling with good news. He pressed a button and waited for her to answer.

"Hey, how'd the table read go?" was her greeting.

"Good. Great."

"I just spoke with Charles Howard."

"Charles Howard." Isaac stopped walking, his limbs lead weights. Charles was an actor's director who had won the industry's biggest awards. Isaac had once landed an invitation to Howard's house after *Brooks Knows Best* wrapped. Just sixteen years old at the time, Isaac didn't know enough to be awed when the man said that *Brooks* was his favorite show.

"He wants to talk to you about a role."

"Talk to me?" Isaac could do nothing but repeat what she was telling him, evidently. "About a role?"

"Yes. I'll let him tell you what he has in mind, because I can't do it justice. But you should be prepared for a drastic life change. Or another drastic life change. This is it, Isaac. What you've been wanting."

"Big break number two," he muttered, feeling both excitement and a touch of dread. He wasn't prepared. Not for either of his "drastic life changes."

"Hey, no pressure," she said as if she'd picked up on his emotions. "Take his call. See if it fits in with your plans."

"Okay."

"Things change. Sometimes in ways we don't expect."

"Tell me about it."

She snapped back into professional mode. "I'll contact Charles's assistant and see what times he has available for the call. I'll text you some options."

"Thanks."

"You're welcome. Congratulations."

He ended the call and stared blindly at his phone. Things changed all right. Everything he wanted in life had been gift-wrapped and handed to him. A woman he cared about, filming the show that marked his comeback, a phone conversation with Charles Howard about a movie role. Those gifts had also come with some unexpected knots. Meghan pretending to be his fiancée with a very real baby on board being the biggest one.

The line between real and fantasy had blurred way too much. Maybe the answer to fixing this was making the fake parts more real. Why should Meghan trust anything he had to say when she was pretending to be engaged to him while wearing a fake engagement ring?

Maybe he could regain control after all. He could make things between them better than ever. Comebacks didn't have to happen solely on screen, they could occur in real life, too.

"That's it," he said to himself, a smile pulling his mouth. He'd given Meghan nothing *real*. No real promise of the future, not even a real relationship. What if he offered to be someone she could count on? Fly-by-the-seat-of-her-pants Meghan was searching for stability. He could provide that for her.

She hadn't been wooed by the promise of fortune and fame, but she liked him a lot. She trusted him. She needed to know that he wasn't going anywhere without her. That she wasn't alone. She didn't have to lean on her sister or her parents when it came to their child. She could count on him.

He would prove to her that he was more than an actor reviving his career. He would show her that he was a family guy, capable of building the life of both their dreams.

Nineteen

Meghan blew out a breath as she exited the doctor's office. Everything was, according to Dr. Singh, "Fantastic!"

She was also *fantastically* pregnant, which she'd known, but was glad to have a doctor's stamp of certainty on it.

They'd found a doctor in Dunn who had been willing to see new patients and, thanks to Kendall's sleuthing, was also discreet about the identity of the patient they were seeing. After Dr. Singh had been sworn to secrecy, Meghan had been whisked in through the back entrance. The building held multiple doctors' offices, but it wouldn't take a genius to figure out why she'd been there.

Doubt rose inside her again. Being responsible for

a human being in addition to herself was a lot to wrap her head around.

"Do you have to go straight home?" Meghan turned toward her sister, who'd accompanied her today.

"Not right away, why?" Kendall slid her sunglasses onto her nose. It was a chilly fall day, but the sun was shining bright.

"You're better with money than me." Meghan was sheepish about admitting that truth, but it was the truth. She hadn't been great at holding on to money after she'd earned it. A new life as a new mom was bound to bring up plenty of unexpected bills and payments. She wanted to be prepared. "Would you help me with a budget?"

Kendall hesitated before opening the car door, watching Meghan over the roof. "What about Isaac?"

It was clear to Meghan that he hadn't changed his plans since this surprise announcement, but… "I'm sure he'll help support his child, but I don't want to count on him. I want to have a plan and count on me."

Something she hadn't done enough of in the past.

Back at Isaac's apartment, Meghan made a pit stop at the deli for an artichoke and mushroom sandwich for herself and a ham and Swiss for Kendall. Upstairs, sandwiches consumed, they were now bent over Kendall's laptop. Meghan didn't love what she saw on the spreadsheet they'd just created.

"This number could change with more sponsors." Kendall tapped the screen. "You haven't exhausted every avenue, you know. I can help."

Meghan eyeballed her sister, who was eyeballing her right back. Kendall wanted to help Meghan grow her podcast and Meghan had been stubborn about accepting her sister's help. She'd wanted to prove she could succeed on her own. Now, though, she was failing to see much of a difference between Kendall introducing her to guests for the podcast and introducing her to potential *sponsors* for the podcast. Plus, Meghan had someone other than herself to think about now.

"I've been hard to deal with," Meghan said.

"What? No, you haven't." Kendall wrapped her arm around Meghan.

"I have. You're trying to help, and I keep refusing you."

"Stop refusing me and I'll add a zero to this number right here." Kendall smiled. "Trust me. I'm a magician."

Meghan had to laugh. "When you swapped Max and Isaac in the Citizen watch ad, that was pretty magical."

"Ta-da!" She snapped her fingers, then wiggled the fingers of one hand, her engagement ring winking in the overhead light. "Even landed myself a fiancé."

A real one, Meghan thought glumly. But she was happy for Kendall and Max, even though Meghan was facing the biggest challenge of her life. Her sister deserved nice things. "How are you making your job work? Being an agent on the East Coast, with your clients on the West Coast, can't be easy."

"I'm going to fly back and forth on occasion, but most everything can be done remotely now. Hell, when

I took the call from Charles Howard's office this morning, they were shooting in Milan."

"Charles Howard?" Meghan's eyes widened. She loved her superhero movies and Charles made the best ones.

"Yep. He wants to talk to Isaac about a role."

"That's amazing! Which one?"

"I am sworn to secrecy." Kendall motioned like she was zipping her lips, locking them and throwing away the key. "But I can say with certainty that it'll involve a lot of green screens."

"What a horrible hint! Every one of his movies requires a green screen." Meghan's excitement overshadowed her worry about her current circumstance for a moment before she felt sad all over again. "If he gets the part, he'll leave for filming for a long time."

Who knew how long. Would he miss three months of her pregnancy? Would he miss his son or daughter being born?

"First off, he doesn't have the part yet. Second, I have no idea when filming begins. You might be celebrating that kid's second birthday by then." Kendall pointed at Meghan's flat stomach. "There's no reason for you to worry about him leaving right away."

"A role in a blockbuster film is his biggest dream come true. It's all he's talked about since I met him. What if...?"

When Meghan didn't continue, Kendall raised her eyebrows. "What if what?"

Meghan wanted their baby to know his or her father.

She knew Isaac well enough to know he cared about his family greatly. He would never go for months on end without seeing his child. But if she continued being stubborn about staying in one place while he was offered a movie role…would he feel as if he had to stay with her instead of pursuing his dreams?

That wasn't compromise. It would be one-sided and unfair.

"Maybe I should go to LA." Meghan chewed her bottom lip in thought.

Kendall's lips compressed.

"If I moved away, I'd miss you like crazy." Meghan turned watery eyes on her sister. "How can I leave you?"

"Honey," Kendall used her wise-older-sister voice. "I shouldn't have said I didn't want you to leave Dunn. It's your choice and you need to do what's best for you, and your baby. Filming schedules end. Movies wrap. Plus, I'm allowed on set. If this was how it worked out, we'd still see each other. Not everyone leaves and never returns."

Which was exactly what had happened to their brother, Quinton. Was the fear of losing someone else she cared about holding her back? Cared… Yeah, right. What she felt for Isaac was so much bigger than "care."

"I'm in love with Isaac," Meghan admitted for the first time out loud. "And I'm terrified he isn't in love with me. I'm scared this has been pretend for him the entire time, while for me, it became real."

"Did you talk to him about this?"

Meghan shook her head.

"He might surprise you. What if he's as crazy about you as you are for him?"

Meghan was afraid to hope that was true, but what choice did she have? Either she put her heart on the line for the sake of love or lived out the rest of her days never knowing what could have been.

It was too big of a decision to make this second, but there was another issue she could handle. "Ken?"

"Yeah?"

"Can you reach out to a few potential sponsors for my podcast?"

Kendall's eyes widened with excitement. "Really?"

"Yes. You're great at what you do, and I've spent too long trying to hide the fact that I don't know what I'm doing."

"Babe, none of us know what we're doing. We're just figuring it out as we go."

"Everyone except you?"

"Especially me," Kendall corrected. "I'd be honored to reach out to sponsors and tell them about my incredibly talented sister."

"Love you."

"Love you." Her sister winked and then began pecking out emails.

Meghan didn't need to prove she could do everything on her own. There wasn't an award given for toughing out hard situations by herself. It was time she started asking for what she needed...and what she wanted. Isaac was the person she wanted. But she didn't only want him close by, she wanted his love, too.

* * *

By the time Isaac returned home, it was dark. The errand he'd run had taken longer than anticipated. He'd hoped to arrive before Meghan went to bed, and he had…sort of.

She was on the sofa, eyes closed, lying on her side with her arm wrapped around a pillow. She was carrying his baby. A baby they hadn't meant to make. A baby he'd be a father to and her a mother. This temporary relationship had landed itself in the permanent category, and even though it'd thrown him for a hell of a loop, he couldn't regret it.

His heart squeezed. He hadn't been great at soothing her worries or making promises about the future. He'd been focused on himself, on his career. He'd been asking her to bend to his needs rather than the other way around. No more. He would provide for his pop-up family, planned or no.

As if sensing him in the room, she batted her eyelashes open, flattening him with those knockout hazel eyes. He shut the door behind him with a quiet click. The only light in the room came from the dim lamp on the coffee table next to her. "Hey."

"Hey."

"What'd the doctor say?" He hated missing her first appointment, but there was no way to skip the script-reading today. Meghan had assured him Kendall was company enough, but he would have liked to be there.

"Everything is fantastic. I heard the heartbeat."

His shoulders sagged. "I missed it."

"We can go back together. I understand your schedule is less flexible than mine."

"You've been nothing but understanding." Which was more than he could say for himself. Being constantly reminded that he was "famous" came with the side effect of focusing on himself. He'd been unaccustomed to putting someone else first.

"How about you?" she asked. "How'd it go today?"

"Good. Great." His head was suddenly jumbled, the weight of the real engagement ring heavy in his leather jacket's pocket. "Actually, I think things could be better. Between us."

She sat up, adjusting the pillow so that it was on her lap. "I think so, too."

Throat full, he sat next to her. "I've been disconnected."

"You've been busy."

"I've let you handle the stress of this pregnancy on your own. It's unfair."

"You're here now."

She was still letting him off the hook. Still looking out for him. Still making herself fit into his mold. She deserved better. He would be better.

"I'm here now," he said. "And now that I am…" He pulled a gleaming diamond ring from his pocket. One he'd had sized while he waited, and waited and waited, at the jeweler's. He'd known what size to request because he'd tracked down the prop master who'd acquired the fake one.

Her eyes were wide on the ring in his hand as he removed the prop ring she wore. "I never gave you a good enough reason to follow me to LA. I failed to acknowledge that what we have started out fake, but Meghan… It's real now. Will you marry me?"

Twenty

Meghan opened her mouth, but no sound came out. It was happening. What she'd secretly wished for was being delivered in the form of a ring and a proposal, this time for real.

He held the engagement ring between his fingers. His expression was one of hope and questioning uncertainty.

There was no need for him to worry. She was in love with him, had decided to follow wherever he went. They could make a family in Dunn or LA, or on the moon for all she cared.

"You want to marry me?" she managed, her smile shaky with excitement. "What brought this on?"

His smile was soft, slightly nervous. She searched his blue eyes for the truth about how he felt about her, watched his lips for the words "I love you" to emerge.

"I never gave you assurances," he said, his eyes on the ring in his hand. "You can count on me. I can provide. I can take care of you and our baby."

He was so sweet to reassure her. Had she done to him what everyone else had done to her? Made him feel incapable? Had she made him believe he'd fall short?

She touched his cheek. "I've been trying to prove to myself that I'm responsible by doing everything on my own. I didn't mean to leave you out. I know you're going to be an amazing father. I've always known that."

He took her hand and kissed her knuckles. "I love hearing that."

Her heart leapt at the "I love" part. She'd thought for a second that he was about to profess his feelings for her. Although, she hadn't professed her love for him, either. The words weren't easy for her to say to anyone other than family members. She understood if he had to work up to it.

"No matter where we live," he continued, "I will make sure you have the best doctors money can buy. I'm going to be there for you as much as I am able. I can't and won't force you to come to LA with me, but I will have to go back at some point."

"Of course you will." She shook her head, her eyes welling with unshed tears. He was offering to let her stay here, to come back for her. He was offering to marry her. She wouldn't go through this pregnancy without him after all.

She threw her arms around his neck, melting into his embrace. "I'm sorry I haven't let you in."

"I'm sorry I haven't been better at this, Meghan. It's

new for me." He held her close, whispering into her ear, "You're amazing."

She pulled away to look into his blue eyes. She'd admired him since she was young, never dreaming of a day when she would meet him in person. Not only had she lived out a fantasy she'd been afraid to hope for, but that fantasy was her reality. After struggling to find her place in life, she'd stumbled into her future. Isaac. Their baby. Their *family*.

"I was going to ask if I could join you in LA, after all," she told him, twining his hair between two fingers. "I don't want to make you choose between your child and your career. And I don't want to be away from you any longer than I have to be."

"You're serious?" He looked the way she felt. Surprised, but overjoyed that she'd come around, the same as he'd just done for her.

She offered her naked left hand. "My answer is yes. How's that for serious?"

"Yeah?" When she nodded, he slipped the ring on her finger and shouted, "Hell, yeah!"

She was in his arms again, his deep laugh reverberating in her ear. "Squire, you and I are going to be the power couple to end all power couples. Wherever I end up filming next, you'll travel in luxury. You and our son or daughter are going to live the best lives. You can count on me."

"I know I can." How had she ever let herself believe she couldn't? She kissed him, unable to stop smiling. Her heart was full, her prayers answered. She needed to be closer to him, to embed this moment in her memory forever. "Make love to me, Isaac."

"My pleasure." He kissed her as he unzipped the back of her dress. His tongue tangled with hers as he pulled the bodice down, and then he glided his mouth from her neck to her collarbone.

She felt everything at once. The ring's weight, this one more significant than the last. His second proposal had come paired with his true feelings and a promise for the future.

"I never wanted you to be temporary," he muttered against her lips as he slipped his hand into her panties. "I wanted you to stay. I didn't know how to ask."

She arched her back as his fingers slipped along her slick flesh. "I forgive you."

He continued stroking her below while his tongue circled one of her nipples. Her belly flooded with longing, and not just the sexual kind. She would have a family of her own. She was no longer alone. No longer wondering if someone would choose her.

Isaac was here. With her. *For* her.

He nipped her earlobe as he tickled her clit with his thumb. "Come for me, Squire."

"Yes," she breathed, as the muscles in her legs tightened. He laid her back on the couch, his mouth on hers, his tongue stroking in and out. Her orgasm crested and rolled, shimmering through her and leaving a wake of warmth that fanned out to her fingertips.

The love she felt for him swelled to occupy every cell in her spent body. In her heart, since before she'd met him, she'd known she'd loved him. She'd known he was perfect, and now he'd gone and proved it.

Lazily she opened her eyes, and blinked him into focus. The boy she'd crushed on, the man she'd made a baby with. The man she would marry. Her life had ended up being the stuff of fiction. She placed her left hand on his cheek. Sexy, scruffy Isaac. She could look into this face for the rest of her life.

"I love you." The words she'd been afraid to say dripped off her tongue like honey, and she watched them fall, waiting for him to return them.

He blinked thick lashes, his eyes tightening at the corners. She'd surprised him. Had he not been able to feel her love for him just now?

"I love you so much," she repeated. The light caught the diamond on her finger, casting sparkles onto the ceiling. "I can't wait to marry you. To have our baby. To spend the rest of our lives together figuring out where to go and what to do next."

A beat passed, and then two. Isaac did not return her "I love you" with one of his own. Tension bracketed his mouth. He loosened his hold on her and sat upright.

He should be celebrating with her. Sliding deep inside of her. Returning her profession with one of his own while they climaxed together. Instead he looked... well, he looked almost nauseous.

One hand went to his face, where he scrubbed his jaw. His eyes were focused straight ahead rather than on her.

She pushed herself to sitting, naked and feeling more vulnerable than ever. Using her dress, she covered her breasts and waited for him to say something. To say anything.

"Isaac?"

"I—I care about you a lot." His smile was pained.

"You care about me," she repeated flatly.

He faced her, adding, "So much," as if that would make a difference.

The veil fell. She saw what she'd missed from the beginning. He hadn't meant the proposal the way she'd taken it. She'd been envisioning true love and happily ever after. He just wanted to...to...provide.

Never before had that sounded like such an ugly word.

Her hand shook as she tugged at the ring. A ring that had ended up meaning even less than the first one had. Yanking it off, she held it out to him. "I've changed my mind."

"What? Don't. Don't do that."

"I thought you meant it when you proposed this time."

"I did mean it." He shook his head, refusing to take the ring. "I just... It was more about insurance and assurances for you. I wanted you to know I wasn't going anywhere. I love our baby and I'll give you both whatever you need."

"You love our baby."

"Of course."

"But not me."

He opened his mouth and then closed it. Finally, he said the words that broke her heart in two. "It's not that simple."

She dropped her hand to her lap, the ring in her grasp as heavy as a cement block.

"We didn't sign up for any of this, originally," he said, "but here we are. We have a baby on the way, and a future that is going to outlast *Brooks Knows Best*. This—" he touched the ring "—is a real marriage proposal. We can have a home—a life—in Los Angeles. I want you by my side."

Tears pooled along the edges of her eyelids. She'd wanted those things, too, but not like this. "In a loveless marriage."

"It's not loveless. There is love here. There is respect. There is sexual chemistry and compatibility. I'm sure as time passes, we'll grow to love each other."

"I love you already. It's not that hard for me, I guess." She shook off his hold and stood.

He'd managed a marriage proposal the *exact opposite* of his twin brother's proposal to her sister. Max had proclaimed his love and dedication to Kendall but had forgotten the "Will you marry me?" part. Whereas Isaac had asked but had forgotten the "I love you" part.

"I changed my mind." She plunked the ring onto the coffee table. What she'd believed was a symbol of forever had been reduced to a symbol of how hard she was to love. "My answer is no."

"Meghan." His voice was gentle. "I'm not saying it won't happen in the future, but right now I have to choose between focusing on a relationship or my career. I'm working to provide the best life imaginable for you and our child."

"Yeah, well, it's not enough." She had accepted less

than she deserved for years. In relationships, in her income level, in her life. She wouldn't compromise any longer. Not with a baby on the way who deserved to have everything. That included a mother and a father who weren't in a sham of a marriage for show. "You know what, Isaac? All the world isn't a stage. This isn't a dress rehearsal you hope to nail later in front of a live studio audience. I'm offering you my whole heart, and if you're too self-absorbed to return it with yours, then you deserve to be alone."

She jerkily tugged on her dress and shoved her feet into her boots. She'd thought the proposal would lead to him burying himself in her body. Them becoming one and celebrating their love for each other. But apparently physically was the only way they'd ever truly connected. He felt nothing for her—or at least not enough.

"This is not fair," he said.

"You're right. It's not fair that I'm the only one in love. It's not fair that you can't allow yourself to love me."

"I didn't say that."

She paused, her purse and coat in hand. "There are a lot of things you didn't say."

She slammed the front door behind her, bypassed Isaac's pink-shirt fan club and walked across the street to the coffee shop. Once there, she hid in a corner and called Kendall.

Twenty-One

Back on set, under the hot lights overhead, Sarabeth delivered her final line on *Brooks Knows Best*.

Her hand was in his, and Isaac poured what might well be the remainder of his energy into delivering his last spoken line of the finale. His costar, her eyes shining, gave him everything he needed.

"Worth a shot, I guess."

The live studio audience went wild. Their cheers and whistles failed to boost his spirits. He was too weighed down by how wrong everything had gone between him and Meghan.

The noise faded into the background as he led Sarabeth down a hallway that ended behind the set. His other costars were there, patting him on the back, whispering their congratulations. In a few minutes they'd return to the stage and take a bow. Hug each other and celebrate the wrap of their reprised roles.

It'd been magical. Everything he could have wished for. Not to mention Charles Howard was calling today. At one point, news that Howard was interested in him had Isaac so excited, he could barely speak. That excitement was still inside him.

Somewhere. Deep, deep down.

At the moment, any remaining excitement or hope was being eclipsed by misery. Not a word he used lightly.

Sarabeth's hand hit his shoulder. "How are you?"

"Never better." He faked a smile, same as he'd done most of the day. He couldn't talk about what was upsetting him. Talking about his and Meghan's relationship ending would reduce him to a whimpering ball of despair. He had to finish strong. This show was the only solace he had left. His best bet was to let everyone believe he was emotional about the show ending. "It's tough. The end of another era, you know?"

"I know." Sarabeth sang her praises of their cast and crew, waxed poetic about the characters she and Isaac had embodied. He nodded while she spoke, but he wasn't listening.

He was thinking of Meghan. The end of their era. He was committed to being a part of his child's life forever, but had lost Meghan in the process. He cared about her, but when she'd mentioned love, he'd panicked. He'd had no idea how to accept the gift she offered. It'd been too much for him to take in at the time.

Max, who had come in for one line the writers added

as an excuse to have him on the show's finale, appeared in front of Isaac like a shadowy gargoyle. He looked unhappy, and Isaac assumed that was his fault. Meghan had left his apartment and hadn't come back. Kendall had come over to collect her sister's things, promising Isaac that she'd be professional, and then warning him not to push her.

"Not now," Isaac said, keeping his voice low. He didn't want to discuss his situation with Max. Now, or ever. "We have to go out and bow."

"Need help pulling your head out of your ass so you can see where you're going?" Max growled.

Isaac, depleted of emotional energy, ignored his brother. They filed onto the set to take their bows, hug each other and wave to the audience. The show's theme song played, and nostalgia hit Isaac hard.

He'd started acting on the show at age five, with his twin brother, before he knew what acting was. Cut to a decade later, he'd extended his time as Danny Brooks as long as possible by doing live appearances. Now, years later, he was on a replica of that same set, his brother by his side.

It was surreal.

His smile was genuine as he embraced his on-screen parents, Sarabeth and finally Max, who pulled Isaac in to give him a thump on the back. Into his ear, Max offered a gruff, "Proud of you, man. You did great work."

Not gonna lie, Isaac had needed to hear that more than he needed his next full breath. Backstage again, they signed one of the set walls with Sharpie markers.

Cecil was there, too, shaking hands with the cast and thanking each of them for making the show a success.

They'd done it. Filming was complete. Max had come back. Isaac had won over his gruff executive producer by plucking a fake fiancée out of the ether. A woman who used to love him, who now hated him. A woman who had radically and permanently changed his future.

"Isaac." Cecil clasped Isaac's hand. "Bring your bride around to my house. Maria and I would love to have you over for dinner. You, too, Max."

Max craned an eyebrow. Isaac accepted with, "Sure thing," even though his stomach clenched at the lie. Would Meghan ever have dinner with him again?

The producer left, and the remainder of the cast broke into small groups. Sarabeth was signing the set wall. Richard was filming it on his phone. Merilyn was hugging Ashley.

"Let's go," Max said, indicating the exit.

"Where?"

"I need a beer. You're going to buy me one."

"Max, I don't—"

"Now."

Ten minutes later they were settled into a corner booth at Rocky's and Max was glaring at Isaac like he'd never stopped. "Why did you propose?"

"Why did *you* propose?" Isaac snapped.

"I love Kendall. I want to marry her. That's why I proposed. Your turn."

Isaac eyed his beer, unsure how much of the truth to tell his brother. He had planned on telling Max what he'd told Meghan. That it made sense to be married for practical purposes. Instead, he said, "Love is complicated."

"It is when the only person you love is yourself."

"That's not fair." Isaac frowned.

He wasn't the villain. He had been trying to do the right thing from the start. He'd been trying to make Cecil happy, to make the show a success, to repair his relationship with Max. He'd been trying to help Meghan's podcast gain a million followers.

Rather than those well-worn excuses, Isaac asked a question he hadn't planned on asking. "What if... What if I did love her? What then?"

"You tell her." Max's eyebrows rose.

"And what if I told her? She'd expect me to be this...whole person. Not to make any mistakes." Isaac gripped his beer glass and shook his head. "She'd expect me to have my shit together."

"What are you talking about?" His brother looked genuinely perplexed. "Loving someone doesn't mean being perfect. It means you're willing to try."

"And when I screw up?" He lifted a hand and dropped it, half embarrassed to admit his fears and half relieved to share them out loud. "Then what?"

"Then you do what you and Meghan have been doing from the beginning. You argue and then you make up."

"How the hell do you focus on a family and a career at the same time? In the past I've been able to handle one at a time. Look at us. I had to choose, and I chose wrong. You and I haven't been the same since. I can't put Meghan through that. Or our child."

Max's eyebrows bowed with sympathy, but his words were loaded with undiluted sarcasm. "Tell me you're not this dumb."

"I care about her," Isaac continued, ignoring his brother's insult. "It's not that I don't care about her."

"Admitting you love her isn't like saying Beetlejuice three times, Isaac. You're not going to summon bad luck because of it. And as for you and me..."

Isaac swallowed thickly, his heart on tenterhooks. He'd long wished he and Max would be close again. That he'd finally cross the chasm between them.

"You're my twin brother," Max said. "It nearly killed me to leave you behind. That's why I stayed in LA for years longer than I'd planned. I told myself leaving LA was for the best, but brother..." Max put a hand on Isaac's shoulder and squeezed. "It was hell losing touch with you. When we finally found our way back to each other, I worried we'd never be the same."

"And?"

Tenderness flooded Max's normally rigid expression. "Look around. We found our way back. You're here, reading my damn mind again. I took the part on *Brooks Knows Best* to be near you."

Isaac blinked. "I thought you agreed to the role for the fans."

"So, you are this dumb."

Isaac wanted to laugh at his brother's joke. He wanted to hug him. He also wanted to rage about the mess he'd made of absolutely everything. Instead he shook his head, remorse his dominating emotion. "I'm sorry."

"No," Max boomed. "Don't be sorry. If I hadn't taken that role you convinced me to take, I might never have realized that while I did the right thing leaving acting, I was dead wrong for holding you accountable for my actions. I never should have cut you out of my life. I never should have left you alone out there or let you believe you didn't matter. You matter more than anyone to me. If I lost you permanently, the way Kendall and Meghan lost their brother..." He trailed off, unable to say any more.

"I feel the same way," Isaac said, his heart aching for an entirely different reason than before. Or maybe the same reason—for Meghan. For how she must have hurt when she'd lost Quinton. For how she must hurt now that he'd proposed to her and made her feel unloved.

"Don't take this the wrong way," Max said. "But you're done using me as an excuse for not taking everything you want in life. Shit changes. That's the one thing you can count on. Nothing will stay the same, and no matter how hard we try, we can't control the circumstances we find ourselves in. You have to roll with it. Do your best. But take the risk, Isaac. If I hadn't risked everything for Kendall, I'd still be alone on this mountaintop, blaming you for my choices. You get me?"

Isaac got him, all right. Some of the ache in his heart dissipated, proving there had been unresolved issues from the years he and Max hadn't spoken. The part of his heart that missed Meghan was radiating with pain, but at least he could see the end of it with him and Max.

"I was this close to having it all," Isaac told his brother. "At one point she wanted to be with me."

"And now?"

"And now she doesn't."

Max said nothing, which was in a way worse than if he'd yelled. Isaac could do without the yelling, but he needed advice. Usually Max hid some advice *within* the yelling.

"I mean, she is at your house…"

Max was already shaking his head. "You can't come there. Kendall will have my ass."

"My family is important. I lost you once. I don't want to lose Meghan."

"So, you thought a proposal would guarantee she'd stick around?"

"Yeah, okay? Yes." Isaac drank his beer, but it sat flavorless on his tongue before he swallowed. "I didn't know what else to offer her."

"You could love her. Let go of the idea that you can't admit how you feel about her until after you've achieved this elusive perfection you've been chasing."

"Wholeness. I've been chasing wholeness," Isaac mumbled, but that sounded as stupid as chasing perfection.

"You can be in love and screw up at the same time. Look at me."

Isaac managed a weak chuckle, but it was short-lived. "Truth?"

"Hit me."

"I… I've been falling for Meghan since the second I saw her sitting across from you here at Rocky's.

I was trying to stick to my plan, do everything in the order I'd decided." He blew out a tortured breath. "I've fucked it up. All of it. Haven't I?"

"Yeah," Max agreed. "But you can un-fuck it up. Admit you were an ass. It's simple, but not easy. I, of all people, understand how hard it can be to tell the one you love how much you love her."

The tightness in Isaac's chest loosened. Had he been fighting the way he felt this entire time because he'd been sticking to a plan? He'd been looking at everything as a goal to be achieved, and in the process had overlooked what actually mattered.

Meghan mattered. His child mattered. Max, and Kendall. They mattered. The accolades didn't matter. He'd been chasing them out of sheer habit.

"So I just...tell her how I feel?" Isaac asked his brother, hope crawling out of the depths and blooming anew.

"In your own way." Max raised his beer glass. "Busting onto a talk show's soundstage is kind of my thing."

"You don't have to be here for this," Kendall said, her finger hovering over the button on her cell phone. She was standing between the kitchen and the back door. "I can take the call outside."

Meghan, seated at the table, rested her head in her hand and tried to appear as if she hadn't been crying every other waking moment for the past four days. "I just want to hear his voice. I won't say anything. You don't have to bring me up."

Isaac's loveless proposal was the nightmare she couldn't wake up from. Meghan's job, as a mother, would be to never paint her child's father in a bad light. She had to get over Isaac, heal her heartbreak and find an amicable middle ground with him. She was hoping it wouldn't take longer than the end of the final trimester to achieve it, but now she wasn't so sure.

She hadn't seen him since she stormed out of his apartment the night he'd proposed with a real diamond ring. He hadn't chased after her, and he hadn't called or texted, either. Unless Kendall and Max were keeping it a secret, Isaac hadn't reached out to them.

Gaining closure required hearing from him, but she couldn't make herself call or go and see him. And since he wasn't calling or coming to see her, that left them at an impasse. She thought maybe if she could hear his voice, hear him as his practical, upbeat self, she could drive that spike the rest of the way into her own heart and begin the healing process.

As much as she told herself she wanted them to be over, there was a part of her that wished she'd said yes to that second proposal. She could be lying in his arms and snuggling close to him…knowing he didn't love her back.

So, okay, that wasn't an option. She refused to marry someone who didn't love her, who'd asked out of obligation. If she thought about that long enough, she could whip herself into being angry, and at this point, anger felt better than grief.

She'd been editing her podcast all week, hoping to keep her mind off Isaac and the fact she'd be raising a baby alone. Well, not alone. Max and Kendall would be there. And her parents had taken the news of their unborn grandchild surprisingly well.

The public, too, had been *gaga* about the baby rumors. Kendall insisted an official statement could wait. Wait for what, Meghan didn't know, but she was glad to postpone it. She felt raw and sad and achingly vulnerable. At least if she heard Isaac and he sounded like himself, maybe she could convince herself he wasn't worth pining over.

"You're sure?" Kendall held up her cell phone.

"I'm falling a bit more out of love with him every day," Meghan lied with a smile. Kendall didn't buy it, her mouth a twist of censure as she pressed the button to call Isaac.

Meghan listened as the speakerphone emitted ring and ring. Her stomach was in knots, and she found herself rooting for his voice mail. He answered in the middle of the very next ring with a casual but definitely not upbeat, "Hey."

"Hi," Kendall replied, her gaze flitting to Meghan. Meghan gave her sister two thumbs-up. "How'd the call with Charles go?"

"Uh. Okay, I guess." He sounded disappointed. Had he not been offered the role? Despite her best efforts to be angry with him, Meghan's heart ached for his loss in addition to hers.

"Oh-kay," Kendall said. "It was my understanding he was offering you the lead role."

"He did," Isaac said. "I turned it down."

He…what?

"You did what? Why?" Kendall echoed Meghan's thought.

"Meghan," he answered.

"You turned down the role for Meghan?" Kendall asked.

"She hates me."

Meghan's heart crushed. She didn't hate him. That was the problem.

"Isaac…have you been drinking?" Kendall asked.

"Don't worry. Max is here. Apparently, he's seeing me home."

Meghan heard Max's telltale grumbling in the background.

"So, yeah. Meghan hates me. Which sucks. I didn't think…" Isaac trailed off.

"You didn't think what?"

"There is no *what*. That's it. I didn't think. I acted. I acted like a dick who had nothing to lose when I told her I didn't love her. I *do*. I just couldn't tell her in that moment that I did. I didn't know how things were going to go. How they were going to work out. I had a plan. I had everything under control."

He was rambling, and Meghan was afraid to read too much into it. Did he admit he loved her?

"Isaac, you should probably talk to her in person. When you're sober."

"I don't need to be sober to know that I love her, Kendall," he snapped.

Oh God. Meghan covered her mouth with her fingers, her insides trembling. She'd been counting on him to be halfway back to his happy self with good news to share about his new film role. Having him drunkenly admit he was in love with her was nowhere in her playbook.

"By the way, this is your fault," Isaac told Kendall. "You didn't tell me the most incredible, beautiful, amazing woman in the world was your sister."

Kendall's gaze softened on Meghan's. "I can't argue with you there."

"She wanted me. Just as I am. Can you believe that?" A humorless laugh cracked through the speaker. Meghan's stomach clenched. "What the hell did she want with me?"

"We don't choose who we love," Kendall answered, a truth Meghan knew to the bottom of her broken heart.

"I had a plan," Isaac continued, almost talking to himself. "Finish filming the show, go home to LA, fame, fortune, blah blah blah. Instead, I'm walking around with an engagement ring in my pocket destined for a woman I don't deserve. Do you think you can talk her into coming to the wrap party? I have to see her. Just one more time before I leave."

"Um…" Kendall made eye contact with Meghan, but Meghan didn't have an answer. She didn't know what to believe. Who was the real Isaac Dunn? The confident man who had arranged his future block by block, or the sad man who had demolished that stack in the name of loving her?

"I'm falling apart, Ken," Isaac said, his voice cracking. "But I'm not giving up. She matters. Her and the baby. Charles Howard can go fuck himself if he thinks he's going to take that away from me."

"Well, um, don't tell him that, okay?" Kendall said.

"Don't worry," Isaac told her. "I know where the blame belongs. On me. This is my fault. I ruined my family once, with Max, and now I'm doing it again. It's what my therapist calls 'a pattern.'"

"Isaac, things will be clearer in the morning. Don't make any big decisions right now."

"Bring her to the wrap party," he said. "Please, Ken."

"I'll see what I can do." Without saying goodbye, she ended the call.

Meghan's hand went to her middle. She was hopeful and sick at once. "Is he going to be all right?"

"You should worry about you," her sister said. "And yes, he's all right. He's with Max. Max always protects the people he loves."

Twenty-Two

It'd taken Isaac a full two days to sober up.

In retrospect, the whiskey shots were a bad idea, but celebrating-slash-mourning with Max had been time well spent. Isaac felt like he'd been hit by a train, but it was a small price to pay to learn that his twin brother didn't resent him.

Healing that rift was an answered prayer, but the circumstance with Meghan was nowhere near resolved. Would she show tonight at the wrap party? Max swore to do his best to try and convince her to come, but had followed that with a warning. He'd told Isaac to have his shit together when he saw her, or else.

The wrap party was at the M Hotel, where they'd shot the majority of *Brooks Knows Best*. There was a red carpet leading into the entrance, complete with a roped-off area to separate the press and fans from the cast. There was a line of limousines on the curb, waiting to deposit the actors from the show.

It was a scene that usually lit Isaac up like a marquee, but tonight, he felt as dim as a burned-out light bulb. From his apartment, he walked downstairs, through the deli that smelled of Italian spices and olive oil, and then across the street.

Screaming fans pressed up against the ropes, holding cell phones and snapping photos, and lifting posters that read "Danny and Rachael forever" and "I love Isaac Dunn!" He waved at the group of ladies wearing pink T-shirts with his face and signature on them. Women everywhere loved him, but only one woman mattered. Meghan had loved him before he'd screwed everything up. Did she still?

"Isaac! Isaac!" His name rippled through the crowd. A photographer asked for a smile. He didn't smile but he did raise a hand to wave. Someone asked where Meghan was—a question he ignored. He tugged on the door handle, spotting Richard in the lobby, when someone else shouted, "Is Meghan pregnant with your child?"

His entire body froze, save for the hand strangling the door handle. Normally anyone could ask anything, and he was able to school his expression, to hide his emotions. As raw as he felt today, a nonreaction wasn't available to him.

Nostrils flaring, he turned his head and told them plainly to mind their fucking business. No fewer than thirty photos were snapped, and no doubt some video. That little sound bite would be on *TMZ* within the hour.

He walked inside, scrubbing his forehead as Richard looked on with concern. "You okay, Isaac?"

He slapped his on-screen father's shoulder. "Not really, Richard. But thanks for asking."

Maybe Kendall could shut this latest publicity snafu down before it grew fangs. He wouldn't stand idly by while those piranhas gossiped about Meghan or their baby. She didn't ask for any of this. Like every other thing he'd done in his life, he'd done this because he'd been selfishly focused on his own career.

He entered the wrap party, wading through a sea of fancy dresses in a rainbow of colors. The men wore tuxes, almost identical to the one he wore—traditional black and white.

He used to tell himself that irrelevance was his worst-case scenario. Could there be anything worse than someone not knowing your name? Now he knew there was something much worse than his ego not being regularly fed. Losing his family—whether it was Max and Kendall, or Meghan and their child— *that* was worse.

He scanned the crowd for Kendall, his gaze snagging on light hair. She stood at the bar, wearing a sparkly purple dress—he recognized it from the photos of the awards dinner with Max earlier this year. He hated to put her on the clock at the party, but the paps were out of control.

He approached, calling out to her while he walked

in her direction. "You have to go out there, Ken. The piranhas are asking about Meghan, and I can't…"

He trailed off when Kendall turned around and he saw she wasn't Kendall at all. His eyes roamed the length of the purple dress, shimmering in the chandelier light, before he reached familiar hazel eyes.

"Meghan."

She ran a hand down the skirt. "I borrowed Kendall's dress. I didn't pack anything fancy enough for a wrap party."

"You look… God, amazing."

She held a clutch in both hands, shielding her belly, even though she wasn't showing yet. Was she still feeling well? Had she told her parents yet? Where had she decided to live? Would she allow him to come with her to the doctor appointments? He pictured her waist growing, her cheeks aglow. Would she sleep with a pillow beneath the weight of her swollen belly in the months to come? He wanted to watch her pregnancy unfold. He wanted to be with her. To love her the way she was meant to be loved.

He just wanted to be there. Wherever "there" was.

"What did the piranhas say?" she asked.

He wanted to kiss her. Tell her he'd been too scared to admit to himself or her how much he loved her. Beg her to forgive him. Beg her to believe him. Where to start?

"You came."

"I did." Her smile was cautious.

Here goes.

"I know you've made up your mind, but you didn't

have all the information. I didn't tell you everything you needed to know, because I was focused on me. On my stupid career." He couldn't be more ashamed of his behavior. "Meghan, I—"

"Isaac! Big congrats on the show, man." A strong hand clapped his shoulder.

"Garth. Thanks. Not now." He ignored the other man's confused expression as he took Meghan's hand and led her away from the bar. He kept walking until they were on the other side of the room, beyond the brightest of the lights, and in an intimate corner.

She was watching him with what might be hope. He wanted it to be hope. *Please, please be hope.*

"I know I screwed this up completely," he restarted. "I'm trying to make up for it. I turned down the role in Howard's film."

"I heard." She frowned. "I'm pretty upset with you about that."

"I know. I—what?"

"You shouldn't have turned down the role. You worked for years to be in a position to take it. I suggest you call him before he casts someone else."

"I— No, Squire, you're not following me."

"No, Dunn, *you're* not following me." She poked him in the chest, coming close enough that he could smell the soft floral scent of her perfume.

He didn't want to talk about his career. He wanted to kiss her. To feel her lips on his one last time. Just to torture himself.

"I love my podcast. It started out as an idea and has grown into more than I ever dreamed. On it, I talk about the shows I loved when I was a kid." Her eyes shimmered, her smile wide. "Your show was a saving grace for me, Isaac. Because you did what you loved, I found refuge in the Brooks family. And in you." She rested her palm on his chest. "Meeting you was a dream come true for me."

This was sounding too final for his taste. "Meghan—"

"I'm not done." Her eyebrows slammed over her nose in a look of irritation. "Dating you was supposed to be a fun pastime. I had no idea we'd end up being so…compatible."

God, they were. He could feel the sexual tension between them this moment. He wanted her, still. More than before, if that was possible.

"I had no right to expect more from your proposal. You were offering to be there for your child, and I shouldn't have—"

"What we had together, physically, was the most intense relationship I'd ever experienced," he interrupted. "I had no idea what to do with a woman who blew my mind in bed as well as while we were sipping coffee on the sofa. You're the complete and total package. You are capable of anything you set your mind to. I knew that. I *know* that." He shook his head. "I'm sorry I wasn't honest with you."

She inclined her chin.

He was terrified she wouldn't believe him, or worse, she would believe him and then tell him he was too late. But as his brother had reminded him, Isaac had to take risks for what mattered.

"I love you." He braced for the feeling of unworthiness, but the only sensation in his chest was stark relief. "I love you, Squire. I wouldn't allow myself to believe it at the time. I was following my own agenda, ticking off boxes in the order in which they were listed. *Brooks Knows Best*, check. Find a fill-in girlfriend, check. Land a movie role…" He shook his head.

He looked around the room, at the guests largely ignoring them. Only Max and Kendall had fixed their attention to the corner where Isaac and Meghan stood.

He pulled the diamond ring from his pocket. "I've been carrying this around with me since you gave it back. I'm embarrassed. I botched this every step of the way. I asked you to do a lot of things you should have been opposed to. You deserve better." His lips pulled into a slight smile. He had no idea what she was thinking. Her flat expression hadn't budged. He forged on even though she hadn't returned the "I love you" he'd delivered. Maybe the best they could hope for was to start fresh. Learn to be friends. Work out a custody situation with their child.

"The proposal was a mistake," he said.

Her mouth dropped open, pain flooding her eyes. He was so glad to see it there, because that meant she didn't agree.

"What I mean is," he said, "the way I delivered the proposal was a mistake. If I were to do it over again…" He held the ring between them. "I'd get down on one knee." He lowered to his knee and looked up at her beautiful face.

Break a leg, Dunn.

"I'd tell you the truth this time around. I'd tell you I don't want you to marry me for the conveniences of a home in LA or great doctors or any of the other crap I said—I will do all of that, but that's not why I want to marry you. If I could go back, I wouldn't let you believe for one second that I was proposing for the sake of the baby. Though, I should warn you, I'm planning on buying many large impractical gifts for our kid no matter what happens with us."

Meghan's lips flinched. *Almost there.*

"I want you to marry me because I love you more than I've loved anyone. Even me," he joked. She lost the battle and gave him an easy smile. "You get me, Squire. In fact, you've *got* me. I may have framed this like a proposal on paper but what I wasn't factoring in was how this didn't work for me unless my heart was involved. I prioritize my passion, and I've never been more passionate than when I'm with you."

He lifted the ring, not taking her hand and making another disastrous assumption. He'd let her come to him. "Forgive me. Marry me. Let me love you. No, you know what? It doesn't matter if you let me love you or not. I do. And there's not a damn thing you can do about it."

Her smile shone, her eyes sparkling like the diamond ring shaking in his grip. "Isaac."

"Don't say anything if you're not ready. Unless it's—"

"I love you, too."

Relief weakened the knees he'd already bent. Had

he won her back? Did she believe him? He stood so fast his head spun. "Yeah?"

"Yeah." She wound her arms around his neck. "You don't have to marry me, Dunn. We could date for a while."

"No deal. I want to make sure you know I'm not interested in going anywhere."

"Except to where Charles Howard is filming the movie you're starring in. By the way…" She put his hand on her stomach and whispered, "We're coming with you."

He kissed her, finally, inhaling her fresh, clean scent. Soaking in the radiance that ebbed off her like a sun-dappled lake. "Marry me, anyway," he murmured against her mouth. "Even though I messed everything up."

"Hmm." She plucked the ring from his grasp, closed one eye and then held it up to the light, turning it this way and that.

"Okay. All right," he said, catching on. "I know what you're doing. It's a real diamond this time. Along with a real proposal and a real profession of love from the deepest, most sentimental part of me. No acting, I swear. This is me. Part-time fuckup, ambitious, fantastic-in-bed Isaac Dunn."

"There's that ego I fell in love with."

"I don't see how."

"You forget." She slipped the ring onto her finger and looked into his eyes. "I've known you for half my life."

"The Danny Brooks version of me."

"There is a lot of you in Danny Brooks, Isaac Dunn. Max was the one phoning it in."

"I heard that," Max growled from behind them, but his beard was smiling. Isaac could tell his older brother was proud of him. Max's approval wasn't necessary, but it felt damn good.

"She's marrying me," Isaac announced.

"Yay!" Kendall whooped.

"If…" Meghan said.

"If anything," Isaac said, meaning it. "I'll move to Dunn. I'll shave my head. I'll take a job in accounting."

"*If* you call Charles Howard right now," she said, "and tell him you made a colossal blunder and then beg him to offer you the role."

"Done." Isaac reached for his cell phone.

"I'll take care of that." Kendall plucked the phone out of his hand. "You two have some celebrating to do."

"Sounds good to me." Isaac buried his nose in Meghan's hair and held on as tight as he dared.

As if she knew he needed reminding, she whispered into his ear, "I love you, Isaac Dunn. I've been in love with you since forever."

He couldn't claim the same, but he refused to be outdone. "I love you, Meghan Squire. I'll spend the rest of forever proving to you how much."

When he dove in for another kiss, he learned their hiding place hadn't been much of one. Whistles and applause lifted on the air around them from cast and crew alike.

"Was that a yes?" Richard, his hands cupped around his mouth, asked.

Isaac looked to Meghan, her crooked smile sending his stomach into cartwheels. "Well, answer the man."

She turned toward the crowd, raised her ring hand and shouted, "That was a yes. Again!"

Epilogue

A black stretch limo pulled to the edge of the street and, amid about a million people—or so his brother had claimed—Isaac, Meghan, Max and Kendall exited the Dolby Theatre and angled for the vehicle.

Flashes lit up the night like fireworks as they climbed into the spacious seats. Once everyone was settled and the doors were closed, Isaac knocked on the darkened window, signaling for the chauffeur to drive.

"How's it feel?" Kendall asked.

"Heavy." Max handed her the statuette he'd won for best short documentary. His submission had barely made it in on time to be considered, but surprise, surprise, Kendall had hustled the package in just under the wire.

She tapped the empty nameplate. "Why isn't your name on this?"

"I was supposed to give it back to be engraved. Didn't wanna." Max shrugged. Next to Isaac, Meghan laughed.

"Well, when we *do* have it engraved," Kendall said, "it should read 'Max Dunn, documentarian, former child actor, father.'"

"Father?" Max gave his wife a shell-shocked blink.

"Yeah. What do you think?"

"What do I think?" Max enclosed his wife in his arms and seared her with a gaze that said he would prefer to be alone with her. "I think it's great."

"Our babies will have a cousin!" Meghan leaned in and hugged her sister, with some difficulty as she was navigating around a large belly.

Thank God she'd come to live with Isaac in California, because there was no way she could have flown in her state. He wouldn't have wanted them to miss tonight for anything. Especially—

"Did you say *babies*?" Kendall asked with a grin.

Meghan feigned innocence. "Oops. Did I say that out loud?"

They'd waited to tell everyone that they were having twins—one boy, one girl. In two weeks' time everyone would know, anyway.

"I'd hoped for your sake they were twins and not one really big baby." Kendall pulled her sister into another hug.

Max slapped Isaac's knee. "Show-off."

"You're one to talk. You beat me to winning an award."

"I'm older. I go first."

"You're only seventy-two seconds older."

"Still older." Max grinned, but Isaac felt nothing apart from immense gratitude. He wasn't jealous of his brother. Max deserved an incredible life. And thanks to Kendall, he had it. That Isaac had been as lucky was a blessing he'd never seen coming.

"Not sure how often they give out the award to actors who portray superheroes, anyway," Isaac said. But award potential wasn't why he'd taken the role in the Charles Howard film. He'd done it because he loved what he did. With Meghan at his side, he felt as invincible as a superhero, so he might as well have the screen credits, too.

"Oh!" Meghan exclaimed.

"Oh?" Kendall repeated. Then she looked down at the floor where a puddle was rapidly forming. "*Oh. Oh!* The hospital! Let's go. Her water broke!"

Isaac stared at Meghan, whose eyes were wide with shock, her hand cradling her belly. It was happening. He was about to meet his children for the first time.

"Isaac!" Kendall shouted.

"Right, I'm on it." He slid the darkened partition aside and instructed the driver to head to the hospital as fast and safely as possible.

"Did you just say 'step on it'?" Max asked with a chuckle as the limo swerved into another lane. "What are you, eighty?"

"Shut up. I'm excited." Isaac moved closer to Meghan and wrapped his arm around her shoulders. She was doing her best to breathe through what he guessed was intense pain. He kissed her slightly sweaty forehead. "Don't worry, Squire. I'm not the only superhero in the family."

She blew out a breath, her gaze locked on him. She was his strength, he was hers. She squeezed his knee, resting her head on his shoulder. "I hope...I survive... this."

"I'll be there the whole time." Caught up in the excitement, and possibly in the middle of a car chase given the limo's speed, Isaac continued his speech. "I'll be around making every moment from here on out the best ones possible. They're going to add up to happily-ever-after—a seemingly unending one."

Kendall's smile was watery. Max nodded proudly, his arm around her.

"Well, this labor...better not...be unending... Or I'll never forgive you." Meghan shot him a glare.

"Goddamn. I love you, Squire."

"I love you, too. Now shut up."

He did, kissing her in between her heavy, uneven breaths.

"Max?" Kendall, who watched her sister warily, asked with a fair amount of concern. "You don't think we'll have twins, do you?"

Meghan's next breath turned into a laugh, and then into a wail of pain.

"Plenty of time to worry about that later, California." Max snuggled a worried-looking Kendall close. "For now, let's enjoy the ride."

Max nodded at Isaac as if to say, *Good job, brother. I knew you'd pull your head out of your ass.*

Isaac's returned nod was the obvious response. *I learned how from watching you.*

You're welcome.

Hell, yeah, he was. Welcome and one lucky bastard, even with Meghan's fingernails digging into the side of his hand. Soon he'd watch his son and daughter come into the world and then they'd all go home and build a life together.

Whether in Dunn, Virginia, or Los Angeles, California, or on a set somewhere in Canada, home was where his wife and kids were.

* * * * *

*If you loved the Dunn Brothers,
don't miss the Dallas Billionaires Club series
from Jessica Lemmon!*

Lone Star Lovers
A Snowbound Scandal
A Christmas Proposition

#2881 ON OPPOSITE SIDES
Texas Cattleman's Club: Ranchers and Rivals
by Cat Schield
Determined to save her family ranch, Chelsea Grandin launches a daring scheme to seduce Nolan Thurston to discover his family's plans—and he does the same. Although they suspect they're using one another, their schemes disintegrate as attraction takes over...

#2882 ONE COLORADO NIGHT
Return to Catamount • by Joanne Rock
Cutting ties with her family, developer Jessamyn Barclay returns to the ranch to make peace, not expecting to see her ex, Ryder Wakefield. When one hot night changes everything, will they reconnect for their baby's sake or will a secret from the past ruin everything?

#2883 AFTER HOURS TEMPTATION
404 Sound • by Kianna Alexander
Focused on finishing an upcoming album, sound engineer Teagan Woodson and guitarist Maxton McCoy struggle to keep things professional as their attraction grows. But agreeing to "just a fling" may lead to *everything* around them falling apart...

#2884 WHEN THE LIGHTS GO OUT...
Angel's Share • by Jules Bennett
A blackout at her distillery leaves straitlaced Elise Hawthorne in the dark with her potential new client, restaurateur Antonio Rodriguez. One kiss leads to more, but everything is on the line when the lights come back on...

#2885 AN OFFER FROM MR. WRONG
Cress Brothers • by Niobia Bryant
Desperately needing a buffer between him and his newly discovered family, chef and reluctant heir Lincoln Cress turns to the one person who's all wrong for him—the PI who uncovered this information, Bobbie Barnett. But this fake relationship reveals very real desire...

#2886 HOW TO FAKE A WEDDING DATE
Little Black Book of Secrets • by Karen Booth
Infamous for canceling her million-dollar nuptials, Alexandra Gold is having a *little* trouble finding a date to the wedding of the season. Enter her brother's best friend, architect Ryder Carson. He's off-limits, so he's *safe*—except for the undeniable sparks between them!

SPECIAL EXCERPT FROM

HHARLEQUIN
DESIRE

Attorney Alexandra Lattimore isn't looking for love.
She's home to help her family—and escape problems
at work. But sparks with former rival Jackson Strom
are too hot to resist. Will her secrets keep them from
rewriting their past?

Read on for a sneak peek at
Rivalry at Play
by Nadine Gonzalez.

"Mornin'," Jackson said, as jovial at 6:00 a.m. as he was at noon.
He loaded Alexa's bag into the trunk and held open the passenger
door for her. "Let's get out of here."

Alexa hesitated. Within the blink of an eye, she'd slipped back
in time. She was seventeen and Jackson was her prom date, holding
open the door to a tacky rental limo. There he was, the object of her
every teenage dream. She went over and touched him, just to make
sure he was real.

"Are you okay?" he asked.

"No," she said. "I was thinking... If things were different back
in high school—"

"Different how?"

"If I were nicer."

"Nicer?"

"Or just plain nice," she said. "Do you think you might have
asked me to prom or homecoming or whatever?"

Jackson went still, but something moved in his eyes. Alexa
panicked. What was she doing stirring things up at dawn?

"Forget it!" She backed away from him. "I don't know why I

said that. It's early and I haven't had coffee. Do you mind stopping for coffee along the way?"

He reached out and caught her by the waist. He pulled her close. The air between them was charged. "I didn't want *nice*. I wanted Alexandra Lattimore, the one girl who was anything but nice and who ran circles around me."

"Why didn't you say anything?"

"I was scared."

"You thought I'd reject you?"

"If I had asked you to prom or whatever, would you have said yes?"

"I don't know," she admitted. "Maybe not...or I could have changed my mind. Only it would have been too late. You would have found yourself a less complicated date."

"And end up having a forgettable night?"

"That's not so bad," she said. "I would have ended up hating myself."

Alexa wanted to be that person he'd imagined, imperious and unimpressed by her peers or her surroundings, but she wasn't. She never had been. She'd lived her whole life in a self-protective mode, rejecting others before they could reject or dismiss her. She now saw it for what it was: a coward's device.

His hand fell from her waist. He stepped back and held open the car door even wider. "Aren't you happy we're not those foolish kids anymore?"

Alexa leaned forward and kissed him lightly on the lips. "You have no idea," she whispered and slid into the waiting seat.

Don't miss what happens next in...
Rivalry at Play *by Nadine Gonzalez,*
the next book in the Texas Cattleman's Club:
Ranchers and Rivals series!

Available July 2022 wherever
Harlequin Desire books and ebooks are sold.

Harlequin.com